THE ENEMY
ADVANCE PRAISE

"*The Enemy* is a *must* read. If ever we are to understand the present by focusing on the past, Sara Holbrook's new novel provides the microscope. It is compelling, accurate, and *hugely* intimate. I lived through this time, as did Sara, hearing World War II stories from my bomber pilot father, but *The Enemy* brings up issues I'd not considered. Hard to put down at *any* age."
—CHRIS CRUTCHER, AUTHOR OF *STAYING FAT FOR SARAH BYRNES*, *ATHLETIC SHORTS*, AND OTHERS

"With skilled attention to the historical detail of 1954, Sara Holbrook paints an intimate portrait of twelve-year-old Marjorie, who learns that wars are caused by hatred, but understanding is the beginning of peace. A brilliant picture of an era that must be remembered so we do not repeat the same mistakes."
—SHARON M. DRAPER, AUTHOR OF *OUT OF MY MIND* AND *STELLA BY STARLIGHT* AND FIVE-TIME CORETTA SCOTT KING AWARD–WINNER

"Spies, commies, and coming to terms with the aftermath of WWII! This is a poignant, fast-paced flashback to how things once were in America, reminding the reader how far we have come, yet bringing pause and thought to how far we have left to go. A worthy debut!"
—PAM MUÑOZ RYAN, NEWBERY HONOR–WINNER AND AUTHOR OF *ECHO* AND *ESPERANZA RISING*

"A stunning historical novel of character, alternately laugh-out-loud funny and deeply disturbing. It has snappy dialogue, a strong plot and stars a sassy, questioning preteen in the red-baiting days of 1950s America. It's sure to bring home honors."
—JANE YOLEN, AUTHOR OF *THE DEVIL'S ARITHMETIC*, *GIRL IN A CAGE*, *OWL MOON*, AND OTHERS

THE ENEMY

DETROIT, 1954

SARA HOLBROOK

CALKINS CREEK
AN IMPRINT OF HIGHLIGHTS
Honesdale, Pennsylvania

Calkins Creek
An Imprint of Highlights
815 Church Street
Honesdale, Pennsylvania 18431
Printed in the United States of America

ISBN: 978-1-62979-498-3
Library of Congress Control Number: 2016951178

First edition
The text of this book is set in Bembo.
10 9 8 7 6 5 4 3 2 1

Design by Barbara Grzeslo
Production by Sue Cole

To my parents: Suzi and Scott
and to my sister Faun.
Most of all, I remember the laughter.

CHAPTER 1

Nazis!

Bernadette and I scream and duck. Crouching behind the wall of our fort, we both grab a snowball in each hand and wait for the attack.

Silence.

Bernadette peeks over the top of the fort and drops back down. It's taken us two hours of rolling and stacking snow boulders and smashing handfuls of snow between the cracks to set the stage for our war. Scarves snake around our heads and mouths, but we still manage to exchange glances.

"Where's Artie?" I ask, pulling my scratchy scarf down over my raw cheeks so I can talk like a normal person and not someone who's being gagged. The red scarf is wrapped around my head three times. My face is probably red, too. Even my lips are chapped. I put the scarf back over my mouth gently.

"I don't want to be a Nazi," Artie screams from behind the garage.

"You have to be a Nazi," Bernadette screams back. "You're the enemy." Bernadette has no trouble talking through her scarf. Her voice would stab through steel.

"I want to be Al Capone," Artie screams.

"You need to be badder than Al Capone," Bernadette yells. "You need to be a Nazi."

"I don't want to."

"You have to."

Artie is Bernadette's little brother. He's only in fourth grade, and we're in sixth, so she thinks she can boss him into anything she wants. Well, the truth is, Bernadette can practically boss anybody into anything. Bossy goes in Bernadette the way gas goes in a car. It's what makes her run and what makes others run out of her way.

Except it looks like Artie doesn't want to be bossed into being a Nazi.

Artie and Bernadette are different in every way. Bernadette's tall for her age and slim with a perfect blond ponytail that never falls. Artie has brown hair that constantly drips into his eyes. Dad says he looks like a fireplug on wheels. About the only thing they have in common is that neither one of them likes to be bossed around.

I am not as tall or as blond as Bernadette, or as stocky as Artie. Basically, I am medium. I rock back on my rubber boots and realize my toes are like stones inside the layers of my socks. No feeling at all.

Artie and Bernadette hurl arguments back and forth at one another. *Yes. No. YES! NO!*

As the fighting continues, I notice a man standing with his hands in his pockets, watching us. It's not Mr. Anderson or Mr. Papadopoulos. On my knees, I crawl to the side of the fort and sneak a look around the side. I squint through my breath clouds. It is not Mr. Ferguson or Mr. Henry. The man is wearing a jacket zipped up to the neck and a black cap with a button on top. It's pulled down so I can't see his eyes. He stands with one hand on his hip, and then he drops it and clasps both hands behind his back.

He's not Mr. Schwartz. Mr. Schwartz has a belly like a beach ball. I would know him a thousand miles away. This man isn't shaped like anyone I've ever seen before. He's thinish and not too tall. The wind blows against his pants, and I can almost see the outline of his legs. A man in a black cap. Just standing and staring.

I know everyone in our neighborhood, and I have never seen this man before. "Hey, Bernadette," I reach to tap her leg, trying to get her attention. "Who's that?"

But Bernadette can't hear me because she's too busy hollering at her brother. I've known Artie and Bernadette my entire life, so I know they can fight like this for hours, even though she usually wins.

"Bernadette!" I whisper-scream.

"Look," I say, and she finally does, but the man's gone. Vanished. Without pausing to even look at me, she hollers, "Artie, you better listen to me, or else."

"No!" Artie screams.

My fingers are cold. I drop my snowballs and clap my hands together.

Bernadette climbs up on one of the fort walls. "Al Capone never had a fort, dumbhead. This is war. We're the good guys. You're the bad guy. That makes you a Nazi." She puts her hands on her hips.

Artie shows himself from his hiding place behind the garage. He pitches a snowball straight at nothing.

"You promised to be the bad guy and you're going to be a Nazi. I said so," Bernadette yells.

"I'm cold," I say. This argument is going nowhere, and I'm molding into an ice cube. I can feel myself getting crispy around the edges. I peer over the fort's wall, my head like a periscope with a pink pom pom on top. But the man's still gone, disappeared as if aliens snatched him up.

"You can't be cold." Bernadette looks down at me. "We haven't even started yet." Frost forms a circle on her scarf in front of her mouth. It jumps up and down when she talks, like a bouncing ball in a sing-along cartoon. She's also wearing earmuffs, and a pointed hat tied in a tight bow beneath her chin. The only part of Bernadette I can actually see are her eyeballs. I know I look exactly the same. Artie, too. In fact, if you lined us up against the wall, you couldn't tell us apart unless you knew our hats.

"Look." I point. Artie is stamping snow off his boots on the Fergusons' back porch and pulling the door open. "Artie's going in." Without saying so, I am glad he's quit because I want to go in, too. I don't tell Bernadette this. It's easier to just let her be mad at Artie.

"Fine," says Bernadette, with a hard clomp of one foot on the soft white snow. "Commie!" she yells at her brother.

"Commies aren't Nazis," I say as I stand up and try to slap away the teeny snowballs grabbing onto my woolen pants as if they've grown roots.

Most commies are Russians. Nazis are German. Commies are communists. Reds. Pinkos. They're all the same thing. Except when the communists are Chinese. Then they're the red devils. But wherever they come from, commies are definitely not Nazis.

"What do you know?" Bernadette asks. "Big zero, that's what. Why am I friends with you?"

"Uh-oh," I say, looking past Bernadette.

"Don't pull tricks on me, Marjorie. Your tricks are as dumb as you are."

There's no use talking to Bernadette when she gets like this, so I just start walking. When I notice that Mrs. Fisher isn't even wearing a sweater, I start to run.

The winter sun, which was bright white all afternoon, is starting to dim. It's been one of the coldest winters since weathermen started measuring snowflake piles and temperatures. Even though it's almost March, it's still cold enough to freeze your eyelashes off. There had been just enough warmth in the sun to make good packing for our snow fort, but clouds are beginning to pull a shade down in the sky. A whiff of night air sneaks inside my coat and down my spine as I hurry.

"Didn't your mother ever teach you that it's rude to walk away when someone is talking to you?" Bernadette calls after me. Then she sees why I'm running, and she starts running, too. We both catch up to Mrs. Fisher at the same time. Her short gray hair is whipping around in the wind and she's wearing a pink, flowered housedress that hangs almost to her ankles. In the clear, cold air, she smells sour, like yesterday's unwashed lunchbox.

11

"Cheese and crackers, Mrs. Fisher! What are you doing out here in your slippers? Where's your coat?" Bernadette tries to take Mrs. Fisher's arm, but she jerks it away.

"Don't touch my baby," Mrs. Fisher cries, hugging her bundle so close to her chest that it almost disappears.

"Nobody wants to take your baby, Mrs. Fisher. We just want to take you home," I say. I pull my scarf away from my face, "See, it's me, Marjorie."

Mrs. Fisher used to call me her little blond angel when I was young. That was before my hair turned the color of playground dirt and she started wandering around cuddling a baby doll. Still, I'm sure she remembers me.

"Have you seen my Tommy?" Mrs. Fisher asks.

"Tommy's not here," Bernadette says. "You have to go in."

"Mom!" We hear Sandy Fisher calling her mother from their front porch.

"Viola! Viola!" Mr. Fisher calls, as he runs up to us from behind. He's carrying an afghan in his hands, and he throws it around his wife's shoulders as soon as he reaches us.

"Where's Tommy?" Mrs. Fisher asks in a soft, crying voice.

"Tommy's gone, Viola," Mr. Fisher says, patting her shoulder.

"Tommy's gone?"

"Thank you, girls," Mr. Fisher says to us. "I'll take her home now."

The snow and dimming light quiet the world so completely that even after we turn toward our houses, we can hear Mr. Fisher talking quietly with his wife.

12

"Tommy's in heaven, Viola, you know that."

"Can't we go get him back?" Mrs. Fisher asks. She is finally letting herself be led home. "Soldiers with guns, can't they go and bring him back?"

Their voices soften into the deepening shadows.

"She's never going to get any better carrying that stupid rubber doll around with her all the time," Bernadette says, and she's not talking under her breath.

"Shh," I say. Even though we are headed away from the Fishers, I'm afraid they can hear us.

"My mother says she's as crazy as a squirrel on gasoline, and it doesn't help that her family just lets her believe that worn-out doll is her Tommy and that he didn't get killed in the war."

"It's not good that Mrs. Fisher just walked outside like that in this weather," I say. Luckily, everyone in the neighborhood keeps an eye out for her. "Last summer when Mom found her sitting on our porch, they had coffee. Mom said Mrs. Fisher might be coming around to be more like her old self."

"Wasn't that the time she went outside in just her slip?"

I shrug. I want to think that Mrs. Fisher is coming around, so I don't answer Bernadette because I don't want to argue. I just want to picture Mrs. Fisher smiling and waving from the porch instead of wandering the neighborhood in a slip, cradling a naked baby doll.

"I'm still mad at you, Marjorie," Bernadette says when we arrive back at the fort.

"Why?"

"You took Artie's side, that's why."

I don't understand why Bernadette's so mad at Artie or me. Russian, German, Chinese. They're all enemies. Italians can be enemies, too, but only if they're Mafia guys like Al Capone. Otherwise, Italians are nice, like Mrs. Lotenero, the secretary at school who keeps butterscotch candy in her top drawer.

Bernadette's mom is Irish Catholic and she has big opinions about people, especially Italians and Lutherans. According to her, Italians are nothing but nasty, ripe olives who smell like garlic. I'm not sure what she has against Lutherans, but she likes to put her foot down about them coming over to her house. We are holidays-only Presbyterians, so she's never put her foot down on me.

As far as I'm concerned, Nazis, commies, or Mafia Italians are all bad enough to have a snowball fight with. Maybe not Lutherans, but the rest are, for sure.

"It's just a snowball fight," I say.

Bernadette's looking at me with skinny eyes.

"This is our best fort ever," I say, not to just change the subject, but because it's true. The snow is packed so solid it's going to be standing until the tulips come up and it shrinks to a white *U* with green grass all around it. But Bernadette is in no mood for standing around admiring our fort.

"You think you're so smart," she says. Bernadette gives the fort a whopper of a kick, but it doesn't move or even crack a little. It's like ice. I can tell Bernadette is even madder now that she's slammed her toe into a frozen wall.

"Ouch," I say. "You okay?"

She is not okay, but she won't admit it. She growls, hands in fists, and limps toward her house and then turns back and points her snow-covered mitten at me.

"You better watch it with your red scarf, Marjorie. People are going to think you're a commie, too."

CHAPTER 2

I put my boots on the rug inside the back door and my coat on the hook. I'm turning toward the hall when Mom yells, "Marjorie, are you trying to flood us out? Put a towel under those wet clothes right now. And put your mittens and scarf on the radiator so they dry by morning."

I put down the towel under my dripping snow pants. The clinging balls of snow have already turned to water and the wool pants are hanging heavy on their hook. My face and feet are tingling as if the air is filled with needles. The house feels hot compared to outside. I shake off one last shoulder shiver—the darkness that had crept into the sunny Sunday afternoon, the stranger in the black cap.

What kind of a man has nothing better to do than stand and stare? Cap pulled down almost to his eyes, no way to see his face? Was he watching us? Looking in windows? Studying the area for a sneak attack? The guy was spooky. But it was like seeing a ghost. If no one else saw him, who's going to believe it really happened?

I take a minute to listen to the house. It sounds as boring as it did when I went outside. A quiet roar leaks out of the living room, which means the hockey game is on. Dad is probably asleep in his chair, or he'd be yelling his head off. I can't go in there. The basement door is closed tight. Can't go down there because of Frank. And there's no privacy in my bedroom. Carol Anne probably has her doll stuff spread out all over the place. Finally, I wander into the kitchen because I've run out of other places to go.

"What's worse," I ask Mom, "a commie or a Nazi?"

"Oh, I don't know, Marjorie. Hand me a potholder, will you?" Mom has an apron hanging loose around her neck. It's untied in the back and swings back and forth in front of her like a pendulum. Mom in the kitchen is a little like Daffy Duck with his tail on fire. Feathers flustered, hands reaching out in all directions, racing in circles.

"Cripes," she screams as she drops a boiling pot into the sink and jumps back. Her glasses are steamed over, and her hair's springing out of its ponytail. I pass her a potholder. She uses it to wipe up the floor.

"I mean, the Nazis and the commies both have dictators and we have a president, I get that part, but what I don't get is—"

"Forget it, Marjorie. The Nazis are all gone. Over. Kaput. Your dad and the other GIs took care of that. Toss a cloth on the table, will you?"

"But—"

"Enough! No more of your questions. Less talking and more helping. Please?"

I specialize in questions. Questions are my thing. Bernadette's brother, Artie? His thing is hives. Things happen, he breaks out in hives. Things happen to me, I break out in questions.

I put both hands on my hips. A familiar frustration starts to growl inside of me because asking questions doesn't always get answers. Like, why does Daddy yell sometimes in the middle of the night? Mom says he kicks in his sleep, too. What's that about? Or why does he wake up out of his chair like a tornado sometimes, his arms whirling in all directions? Or why did I find Mom just standing and staring out the window last week?

"Why are you just staring like that?" Seemed like an obvious question to me, but did it deserve an answer? Nope. All Mom said was, "Service under fire," which basically meant *none of your beeswax*.

That's the sad truth about me asking questions. Basically, nobody tells me anything.

My hands drop to my sides. "What's for dinner?" I sigh.

"Creamed chipped beef on toast," Mom says as she struggles with the can opener, trying to pierce a can of peas. "Mashed potatoes and . . . oops," she yelps, peas flying.

My shoulders slouch. Another dinner of soft foods. Daddy's gums must be bleeding all over the pillowcases again. The bleeding makes Mom nuts because she has to soak the pillowcases in detergent and bleach in the basement, and sometimes I have to go down and give them a stir with the broom handle. That's all because Daddy got trench mouth fighting the Nazis, which is also why we have to eat soft foods. I don't mind stirring the pillowcases, but I do mind eating mushy food every night of the week. But not only does no one ever tell me anything, no one ever asks for my opinion, either.

"Don't give me that look, Marjorie. Be a doll. Silverware on the table, and then call your sister. And ask Frank if he's joining us for dinner."

"How about I ask Frank to find someplace else to go for dinner?" I mumble as I jerk open the silverware drawer.

"Marjorie!" Mom whispers. "Now, you stop that this instant." She aims a wooden spoon at my face and leans in close, "It's been almost a year. It's time you just accept what is, young lady. You know that boy has no place else to go." She puts the spoon in her mouth like a pirate's knife and dumps the can of peas into a saucepan on the stove. She strikes a match, turns on the burner, and stands back as she lights the gas. The burner explodes in a burst of flames. "Cripes!" she exclaims again, tossing the used match in the sink.

"Too bad." I walk into the dining room with two fists full of silverware as I hear Mom hissing my name again, telling me to keep it down and how she just doesn't know what's gotten into me this year.

If she just looked in the basement, she'd know.

It's one thing to get a younger brother or sister. That's normal. That happens to kids all the time. I have a friend, Mary Virginia O'Donnell, who's in my sixth-grade class, and that's happened to her every single year since kindergarten. There are eight kids in her family and Mary Virginia's the oldest. I don't remember ever seeing Mrs. O'Donnell when she wasn't expecting.

But waking up one day and finding out, *poof*, you just became a little sister to a teenage weirdo overnight is not normal. And

19

the fact that he's a senior in high school who owns a motorbike and a leather jacket is even more zonko. At first Mom said she wanted to draw the line at the motorbike when he moved in, but Dad said to let him have it. "Boy is sleeping on a borrowed bed in a borrowed house with a borrowed family. Let him have something that's his."

In the beginning I felt sorry for Frank because of the way things happened with his pop dying and all. It was really sad. The four of us went to his pop's funeral, and after the service, we became a family of five because he came home with us. Frank already has a brother, but he couldn't come to the funeral since he's in prison for borrowing a car without permission. Dad says they call that stealing in his book, but Frank says Dad doesn't understand. Anyway, Frank was all alone, standing outside of the funeral home with a suitcase, and then he was part of our family.

That was the first time I ever heard someone's death described as *not by natural causes*. Turns out, *not by natural causes* is not something you're supposed to ask questions about at a funeral. But how was I to know that? I'd never been to a funeral before. Even though Mom made me go sit in the car, I still felt sorry for Frank. At first.

But then after a couple of months he started teasing me and bossing me around like a real brother. Not the kind of brother that gives you advice on what's cool, or as Frank would say, *what's hep*. He turned into the always-in-my-business, thinks-he-knows-everything, bossy kind of brother. That's when I started hating him. Really hating him.

I arrange each place setting on the table, making sure the knife blades point away from the plates. Mom goes crazy over dippy details like that. Knives pointed the wrong way, forks on the wrong side of the plates, glasses on the left side—that stuff makes her nuts. There is enough mess in this world, she says, that she doesn't need to sit down to it at dinner. As I finish rounding the table, putting down the silverware just right, my little sister, Carol Anne, comes bouncing down the stairs.

"I hope you weren't touching any of my stuff," I say. We share a room, Carol Anne and me. Frank sleeps on a bed in the basement. It's not a real bedroom, but Dad says it's the warmest place in the house, which is true since it's next to the furnace. The furnace is the same color as the coal that Dad shovels into it, and it'll burn the skin right off your hand if you touch it. Frank tried to tape a picture of a girl in a bathing suit to the side of it when he first moved in, and the tape melted and the picture turned brown and curled up like a dead water bug, which Mom said was for the best anyway. All I know is that furnace belches fire like a dragon when someone opens the grate.

When I was little, Dad convinced me that the furnace was a monster and that he was its trainer. He keeps the furnace monster happy by feeding it coal, but he said if I ever touched it or came near it when he wasn't around, the fire-breathing monster would eat me alive. I believed him, too. Just like Carol Anne believes him when he tells her that he was in the cavalry and his vaccination scar is where he was shot in the arm with a flaming arrow by Sitting Bull in the war.

My dad was in the big war, World War II. He was in some war in Korea, too, but that was just a little war. I don't know what that was about, really. But the big war was about beating the Nazis and the Japs, who as far as I can tell, decided to gang up on us at the same time. Anyway, all those wars are over. Now we have something called a Cold War. I'm not sure what that one's about either, but it has to do with the H-bomb.

"Marjorie, wake your dad up. Time to eat," Mom calls from the kitchen.

I may not be the oldest kid in the house anymore, but at least I'm not the youngest. I immediately tell Carol Anne, "Go wake up Dad."

"No!" she screams. Her eyes get all wild and wide and she knocks over a chair diving under the dining room table as quick as a chipmunk darting into a hole. "No. No. No. You can't make me," she calls from under the table.

"Oh, grow up," I say. "Stop being such a baby."

"No, no, no, no, no," she whines. I don't even have to look. I know she's rocking back and forth.

Before I can pull her out and point her toward the living room, a stretching shadow appears in the doorway.

"What's going on in here?" Dad says.

"Daddy!" Carol Anne squeals and scrambles out from under the table and springs into Dad's open arms. Dad tosses her over his shoulder and bends down to pick up the overturned chair, with Carol Anne laughing and beating on his back.

"You two get jobs yet?" he jokes.

Do we have jobs, and have we found husbands yet? Those are two of Dad's most worn-out things to say. He isn't serious, of course, since I'm twelve and Carol Anne is six, and he doesn't even want Mom to have a job. Every once in a while Mom checks out the *Help Wanted, Female* section of the newspaper. There's never anything listed except jobs for receptionists and bookkeepers, and Dad says he doesn't want his wife being someone else's flunky. I'm pretty sure he's serious about that part.

"I saw you and your friend out there holding down the fort, Marjorie. Keeping the enemy at bay?" he laughs, setting Carol Anne on scrambling feet. She takes off like a wind-up toy into the kitchen.

"We had to take Mrs. Fisher back home," I say.

He shakes his head. "Sad case, that one."

"And some guy I never saw before was watching us. He was wearing a black cap."

"Black cap, eh? Ya hear that, Lila?" he calls out to Mom. "Spies in our midst."

Spies? I feel my eyes growing and then I remember not to be a patsy. You can't believe what my dad says half the time. But sometimes I do and then he says, "Don't be a patsy, kid," which basically means, *Don't be a dumbbell; he's just making stuff up again.*

Dad was in the cavalry in the war. That's a true thing. He just rode a tank instead of a horse.

Daddy doesn't talk too much about the war except to make jokes. One of his favorite jokes is about this time when his feet got frozen and he lay in a hospital bed for two weeks while the

23

doctors decided if they were going to cut his feet off. He says the nurses were taking turns trying on his boots because the army sent them into combat in saddle shoes and cotton dresses, and they had to dress themselves in jackets and boots wherever they could find them. They mostly just took boots and stuff from GIs who didn't need them anymore. Mainly dead GIs.

Daddy says that one day he just stood up and walked out of that hospital and said, "Sorry to disappoint ya, gals." That whole story is true. I think.

I hear Frank's feet stomping up the wooden basement steps.

Frank.

What do you make of a guy who greases his hair and leaves his collar up, trying to be cool even at Sunday dinner? I give him a look that says exactly how cool I think he is—exactly not one bit.

"I think the Red Wings are going to go all the way this year. You should've come up for at least part of the game," Dad says to Frank.

"Big exam tomorrow." Frank plops in his chair and picks up his fork. "Bunch of nothin' if you ask me. I can't see how memorizing the chemical elements is going to help me when I join up in June." Mom waves her napkin in his direction, motioning him to put his napkin in his lap.

"Got to graduate," Dad says. "It's a new day. Got to get the piece of paper if you want to get anywhere in the military today. Besides, your pop wanted you to graduate, boy. You know that."

Mom clears her throat and straightens the napkin on her lap.

"Frank, have you ever thought about college?"

Everyone's hands and mouths stop moving as we look at her.

My mother's a college graduate.

It's true.

It happened during the war because her daddy didn't want her hands turning dirty in a factory helping the war effort, so he sent her off to a safe place with ivy all over it. She never lies about going to college, but she doesn't bring it up either. Probably because, like Dad says, it doesn't help her do the dishes any better than the next woman. It's almost a family secret, like a birthmark or my grandpap's horse-thieving uncle who had his name cut out of the family Bible. Something we don't talk about.

"It's not out of the question, Frank." She straightens her knife, making it perfectly parallel with her spoon. "You are a bright boy."

"Leave it, Lila. College ain't the be-all and end-all," Dad says, reaching for the salt and restarting his dinner. My dad practically never says *ain't*. I know he just said it to get under Mom's skin. By the red flush of her face, I can see it worked.

Sometimes when he's under her skin it makes her laugh, like the time he stole her bra off the clothesline and wore it like earmuffs. But she doesn't laugh this time.

"Chemistry's not my thing, that's all." Frank's all hunched over, scooping up food. Mom sits up a little straighter in her chair. She watches Frank, and I know she wants him to sit straighter, too. I sit up as straight as I can to try and take her mind off of him as he continues to go at his food like a gorilla.

"Who cares that according to some book, the letter *C* stands for carbon and *OX* stands for oxygen. Like it's too much trouble to just say 'carbon' or something," he mumbles into his plate.

"*O* stands for oxygen," I whisper under my breath.

"What's that, punk?" Frank shoots back.

"Peas, anyone?" Mom asks.

CHAPTER  3

Monday is Monday. Alarm. Bowl of cereal. I check the temperature on the thermometer hanging outside of the window. Twelve degrees. I pull on a pair of flannel-lined corduroys under my skirt for the walk to school so my kneecaps won't freeze off. It doesn't seem fair to me that boys are allowed to wear pants to school while girls are given the privilege of chapped legs. I mean, who wrote that rule? If I don't wear pants under my skirt, my legs freeze up and feel like they're going to crack right off, so I'll be walking on bloody stumps. I tuck my pants into my boots and don't care how it looks.

"I'm going to borrow this, okay?" I call to Mom as I grab her green scarf.

Mom's bent over the newspaper and her crossword puzzle, chewing on the end of her pencil. "What's the matter with that beautiful red scarf that Grandma Mona knitted you for Christmas?" she asks, but I can tell she really doesn't care.

"Still wet," I lie, wrapping her scarf around my head twice. Bernadette will be waiting for me on the corner, and while she's probably over being mad at me, there's no use waving a red scarf in her face. That's like inviting her to call me commie for the rest of the week or forever. Bernadette is the most popular girl in both classes of the sixth grade and also my best friend. Partly we are friends because she lives next door, but also because I know how to be friends with her.

"C'mon," Bernadette says when she sees me, and then she's silent. We are halfway to school before she huffs, "I can't believe you wear those baby pants under your skirt." She's wearing a plaid skirt and knee socks. For sure her skirt is scraping her raw, and her frozen knees must be on fire. I know this because I've tried it. Bare knees in this kind of weather cause real pain.

"You have to grow out of wearing those pants before junior high next year, Marjorie, or I'm not walking to school with you anymore."

I don't say anything. Not a word. We've walked to school together every day since kindergarten. Usually Bernadette does most of the talking and I do most of the listening. I know how to wait out her anger, and if I just let her grumble along and don't say anything, she'll be out of steam by recess. Then we can be back to being best friends, just like normal.

After we take our seats in class, Mrs. Kirk announces that tomorrow a new girl will be joining our class, and she's not from here. She's from another country, Canada. Mrs. Kirk stares at her grade book for a while like she's studying a map. Then she says the new girl will be sharing my desk.

Bernadette speaks right up. "I can share with Marjorie," Bernadette offers, sounding sweet as a Hershey bar. Mrs. Kirk shakes her head. "You two chatterboxes?" She laughs. Then she tells us to pull out our grammar books and rulers.

Bernadette slaps her book on her desk to send a telegram to the world that she's not happy. I can see that her mouth is pinched tight.

I turn my eyes to my book and smile. *Good,* I'm thinking. *Now she can be mad at Mrs. Kirk, and she won't have time to be mad at me anymore.*

A new girl.

From Canada.

I feel a little excitement inside. I wonder what she will look like and if she will smell like garlic or wear big petticoats. The new girl will make us a class of thirty-eight kids with thirty-two desks. Five rows of six desks and one desk sitting in the back corner and one right by Kirk's desk. Those are the desks where Owen Markey and Danny DiMario sit until they learn to control their actions.

Our school has only two sixth-grade classes and five first-grade classes. Kirk says we need another sixth-grade classroom, but there's no chance because there are even more kindergarteners coming in next year.

I saw a picture in *National Geographic* of a snake with a bulge in it because it had swallowed a whole rabbit. Homer Elementary School is like that snake, and Carol Anne and her class are the bulge, part of a boom of babies who were born right after World War II. All the GIs who didn't get killed came home, got married, and had kids. Bing, bang, boom. And those who were already married, like my mom and dad, had more kids. Homer Elementary is so crowded, it has one staircase for going up and one for going down, with an indoor safety patrol to make sure no one tries to go the wrong way and winds up being stomped to death.

National Geographic is my school away from school. I like the articles about snakes curled around tree branches in Brazil and crocodiles floating in the Nile and little gorilla babies, which are about the cutest things you've ever seen. I study the pictures of howler monkeys and cockatoos and pretend they are on the branches outside my window. But what I really like, what I dream the most about, is someday visiting the places where all the animals live, places where everything's not the same as it is here.

When the clock finally tick-ticks its way to 3:15, we stand in the cloakroom and bundle up for the walk home.

"Look," says Bernadette, with excited eyes. She holds out a nickel. "How about I call my mom and tell her we're going to stop at the library on the way home? You have any money?"

I show her the nickel Mom gave me this morning.

"Good. I'll make the phone call, you buy the doughnuts," Bernadette says, pulling her ponytail out through a hole in the back of her hat.

"You want to come over?" Mary Virginia asks Bernadette, but she shakes her head and says, "I'm busy."

She could have invited Mary Virginia along, but she doesn't, which just goes to show that even though I make Bernadette mad sometimes, I'm still her best friend. I button up my coat as quick as I can and follow her to the pay phone by the staircase.

Since my nickel is in charge of buying the doughnuts, I can

keep the change. Cream-filled doughnuts at Schwartz's Bakery are three cents, but a nickel will buy a couple of two-cent fried cakes. I'll have a penny left over. That means if Mom gives me a nickel tomorrow, I'll have six cents, and I can buy cream doughnuts for Carol Anne and me after school.

Most people hate Mondays, but they're my favorite. Monday is the day Carol Anne has Camp Fire Girls and I don't have to walk her home, even though it seems weird that there is a day I don't have to take care of her.

It's mostly weird how Carol Anne is starting to have her own life now that she's in school. Before then Baby Carol Anne never seemed real to me—the kid in the high chair, the sleeping kid who's the reason everyone has to whisper, the lump who's allowed to sit on Mom's lap in the front seat or on the sofa.

Mom said the other day that Carol Anne needed new shoes and Carol Anne just nodded and said, "I'm losing my littleness." Losing her littleness is something that can't happen too fast as far as I'm concerned, which is why Monday's the best day of the week.

So Bernadette's nickel clangs its way through the pay phone in the school lobby and my nickel drops down onto the glass counter at Schwartz's.

"How are you two darlink's doing today," Mrs. Schwartz asks as she gives us our fried cakes on paper napkins.

Bernadette answers for both of us. "Just fine. Thank you very much for asking. And how's your husband?"

How's your husband? I look at Bernadette like she's just turned into a Martian. Where does she come up with these things? But what I really can't believe is how grown-ups talk back to her and take her seriously.

"Ah, my sveet. Mr. Schwartz ist vell. Gone home to bed, you know. He poured deez doughnuts at two o'clock dis mornink."

"Two o'clock? Gee. That's so early." Bernadette opens her eyes as wide as two crullers.

"Ev'ry day. Ev'ry day." Mrs. Schwartz smiles and hands us two free doughnut holes on another napkin.

The cold air takes our breath away as we step back outside.

"I can't believe you," I say.

"What do you mean?"

"*How's your husband?*"

"You're just too shy. You should speak up once in a while and maybe you'd get free doughnuts," Bernadette says. "Darlink," she imitates Mrs. Schwartz's accent perfectly. "You can't go through your life like a ghost."

"I am *not* shy," I say. I hate when she says that. It makes me want to kick something. "And I'm not a ghost."

"Not with me, you're not. Just with the rest of the world. Here." Bernadette hands me my free doughnut hole. We eat the doughnuts in a few bites as we walk, bending into the cold wind.

"Do you believe there's such a thing as spies?" I ask.

"Real spies or movie spies?"

"Real ones. You know, like that guy yesterday in the black hat."

"I didn't see any guy in a black hat."

"Well, I did, and he was kind of—I mean, *really* staring at us. You didn't see him?" The wind swooshes a cloud of snow up from the sidewalk right into our faces. We grab on to each other's arms and trudge along together.

"Why would anyone want to spy on us?" asks Bernadette when she gets her breath back.

She has a point. Spies probably have better things to do than stand in the freezing cold and watch three kids fight about Nazis.

"But *what if*? That's all I'm saying. What if he's a real spy, and he's watching us. In our midst." Every day the newspapers and the television warn us to be alert for spies and commies in our midst. "Midst means right in our neighborhood, Bernie."

"I know that. You're the one who answered, *C. light rain,* for *midst* on the vocabulary test. Kirk read it out loud to the class, remember?"

I give her a swat on her arm for remembering that. We both laugh.

"But seriously, he could be watching where we live."

"For what?"

"Spy stuff. I don't know."

"If you're so worried, why don't you tell someone?"

I want to scream at her that I *had* told someone: I'd told her. I'd told my dad. *And* my mom knew. But no one was taking me seriously. If I were Nancy Drew I'd find a way to investigate him and probably catch him in the act. Turn him over to the cops. I'd be a hero.

"I'm not as shy as you think I am," I say.

"Right," Bernadette says as she inches the heavy library door open.

The library's a warm envelope made of golden wood. Tall windows gather every bit of light out of the winter sky and project it in streaks across the two main rooms. Every blank wall is heavy with books, and the floor sighs with each step as we cross it. We brush the snow off of our boots on the rug by the door and tiptoe in, trying not to make a sound, as if we are tracking deer in the forest. I wince every time one of our rubber boots squeaks.

One of the million things that Bernadette and I share is our gigantic love of books. All books. Picture books. Stories. Biographies. Encyclopedias. Even the unabridged dictionary that sits in the library on its own stand is something we've spent time studying. This library is as familiar to us as our own homes, since we spend at least one afternoon a week here, and almost every Saturday morning. The only problem is, now we're in sixth grade. Technically we're too young to be let into the adult section, even though we've pretty much worn out the children's section.

Mom started bringing me to story hour when I was hardly big enough to stand and walk at the same time. As soon as I was able to come here with Bernadette, Mom stopped making trips to the library because she's always too swamped with all the Mom stuff she has to do.

Bernadette and I do our Nancy Drew best to break out of the kids' section every time we visit. We act casual and try a right turn into the grown-up area instead of the left turn into the children's area as we enter the library. The checkout desk stands between the two, and our chance of snagging a copy of *Life* magazine or a biography, instead of re-reading Laura Ingalls Wilder again, depends directly on who is standing behind that desk. Mrs. Svenson will often pretend to be looking the other way.

"Ladies!"

Mrs. Pearson is standing behind the desk with her arms folded tight.

Rats.

"Ladies?" She eyeballs us with a beady, accusing stare over her glasses and points to the CHILDREN'S AREA sign.

"Oh, hello, Mrs. Pearson. How are you doing today?" sings Bernadette in her sweetest voice.

"Children's area," Mrs. Pearson says again and nods to the left.

"Of course, Mrs. Pearson. Thank you so much." Bernadette smiles as she whispers, "Witch" under her breath. We obediently make the left turn.

The smell of the cold is still on our coats as we sling them over the backs of two chairs at a pint-sized round table. "We don't even fit in these chairs anymore," Bernadette moans.

"That ought to be the rule. You outgrow the chairs in the children's area and you outgrow the whole room," I say.

As if we are acting in a play, we know where we go next. Straight to the magazine section to see if a new craft or puzzle magazine has arrived. Not as interesting as the *Life* or *Vogue* magazines in the adult rack, but better than picture books.

"What's that doing there?" Bernadette stops short. A rolling cart of books is shoved up against the wall by the magazine rack. Adult books. Just sitting there.

"Quick," I whisper, and we each grab one and slip it into a copy of *Highlights* magazine as slick as sticking salami into a sandwich—a big, fat, overflowing Dagwood sandwich. "This way," I motion, and we hold the barely wrapped books tight to our chests and smuggle them to a back table, out of the direct line of sight of nosy Mrs. Pearson.

"What'd you get?" Bernadette asks after we sit down.

"It's just a number," I say, reading the title. "A date. *1984*. What's yours?"

"*The Grapes of Wrath*," she whispers back. "Mrs. Pearson will never let us check these out."

"Read fast," I answer, opening the cover.

"Easy for you to say," Bernadette says. "Your book is a number, and you're good at numbers."

"Shh."

CHAPTER 4

Caught in the act.

I sit slumped in a baby chair Mrs. Pearson has pulled out of the children's section and set by her desk where she can keep an eye on me.

"Are you all right, Marjorie?" My mother swooshes up to the front desk, looking like she rode in on a tornado. Her French twist has untwisted and half of her hair is tucked behind one ear. Her face is a blotchy tomato color from the cold and her unbuttoned coat falls loosely from one shoulder. Hanging looped around her neck is my red scarf.

I nod. Mrs. Ferguson already picked up Bernadette. She promised Mrs. Pearson to ground Bernadette from books for weeks, or months, or maybe even years. She made a big deal about ordering Bernadette straight into her car. She announced to the entire library that she was going to wait until Bernadette's father arrived home to give her a good talking to. "There are certain things you have no business knowing about at your age, young lady," she had said, looking straight at me and buttoning up Bernadette's coat like she was a doll or a five-year-old instead of what she is, which is usually anything but quiet.

Then she snapped Bernadette's earmuffs on a little snappier

than necessary and pulled her hat down over the whole business and most of her eyes. "You are certainly not going to bring any communist propaganda into my house, Missy, I will not permit it. Do you hear me?" I doubted Bernadette could hear anything with earmuffs, a hat, and a scarf covering her ears, but the rest of the library could. Mrs. Ferguson made sure of that.

"Not when your father is heading up a committee at the Rotary to investigate communist threats in the community, no sirree, little lady." She grabbed Bernadette by the shoulders and turned her around. "You will grow up to be a lady, which means you will not be reading filth." She gave Bernadette a swat on her behind, and Bernadette started walking toward the door like a robot. Mrs. Ferguson said, "Thank you, thank you," about a dozen times to Mrs. Pearson. She thanked her for her patriotism and her diligence. And then she thanked her on behalf of her husband and the entire Rotary Club for being "ever vigilant." Then both of them shook their heads and clucked their tongues all over the place.

"We can't be too careful about the communist threat," Mrs. Pearson said.

"You are entirely right about that. Get moving into the car," she prodded Bernadette, who was dragging her rubber boots across the floor. She paused. "I brought the blue car," she called out, bringing the total to three times she had managed to let it drop that they are a two-car family. She walked away, running her fingers back and forth over her pearl necklace.

Bernadette's dad was 4-F during the war, meaning he couldn't fight because he had bad feet. Instead of fighting, he did his part in the war effort by making Jeeps for Ford. Dad says that puts the Fergusons ahead of the game while the rest of the GIs have to play catch-up. That explains why they have two cars and one of them is a 1953 custom red Crestline Sunliner Ford-O-Matic with a convertible top, and we have a basic DeSoto that's four years old. Mom likes to say, "If you can't say something nice about a person, you shouldn't say anything at all." She also says that any woman who wears pearls to drive to the grocery is a little too full of herself, even if she does own a convertible.

My mom doesn't have her own car. She had to walk to the library to pick me up. I know this is going to make things a hundred times worse for me than for Bernadette. I stare at the floor and wait for the ceiling to open and dump a ton of bricks on my head.

Mrs. Pearson has her arms crossed tightly, the way she always does. Crossed arms are as natural to her as breathing. It makes me wonder how she opens a car door or flushes a toilet. I imagine she was born with her arms crossed, telling the doctor to keep it down as soon as she opened her eyes.

Whatever she does to wake up cranky every morning before work, she does it perfectly. Mostly she's supposed to circulate around with her coffee breath and look over kids' shoulders to see what we are reading, but she's usually too lazy to leave her swivel chair. She relies on her little spies. She has a gang of second graders who are her library monitors. They do her dirty work, reporting back whenever they see any of the rest of us talking or reading something we managed to sneak out of the adult section. You might wonder what's in it for them, but the truth is, second graders will do anything to please a grown-up. Hillary Hastings was the one who caught us, and she shot like an arrow up to the desk to tattle to Mrs. Pearson.

Here's the joke. In the first two pages of this book *1984*, this guy Winston is walking up the stairs to his apartment. Hanging on the walls are these telescreens that work something like a television and something like a camera. While Winston watches the person on the screen, that person is also watching him. The watcher is this guy called Big Brother, and he watches Winston's every move.

So, I'm reading about this Big Brother and how Winston is being watched, when really it's me who is being watched by Hillary Hastings. Except unlike Winston, I don't know I'm being watched until it's too late. And now Mom, Mrs. Pearson, and Mrs. Svenson are all watching me. I may be the most watched kid on the planet. My feet want to shift around, but every part of me except my bouncy knees is afraid to move.

"What exactly is the problem here?" Mom's breathing hard. She only glances at me. Mrs. Pearson is obviously the person in charge.

"Your daughter was reading *this*," Mrs. Pearson says and lifts her crinkled nose in the direction of the closed book like she's pointing out a skunk that's just crawled out from under the desk. Her lips are pressed together as tightly as her arms are folded.

"What?" Mom asks, her eyes darting all around. There are books on every wall and surface, and she has yet to focus on *the* book.

"This book." Mrs. Pearson temporarily unwraps her arms and taps it with one fingernail, then quickly locks them back into their natural, crossed position. "This book is a pro-communist manifesto that's been pulled from the shelves for the safety of the public, and your daughter just decided to help herself."

"Oh, for cripes' sake." Mom drops her elbow onto the checkout counter and sinks her forehead into her open hand for a second. Then she stands back up and puts both hands on her hips. "I practically ran all the way here. I thought something had happened."

"Clearly something *has* happened, Mrs. Campbell. And you might as well know that she encouraged her little friend Bernadette Ferguson to steal a book that's even worse. Not only is your daughter a thief, she is an instigator, Mrs. Campbell."

"A thief?" Mom starts shaking a little, but it isn't because of the icy temperature outside anymore. Nope. Her eyes narrow and she takes in a slow breath. She may have been cold a second ago, but one look at her, and I can tell she's all heated up now. "The girl has a library card. I don't think you call it stealing when she borrows a book."

"Shh," says Mrs. Pearson, letting Mom know who's boss. Her eyes circle all around Mom, taking in her messed-up hair, her flyaway coat. Her eyes catch on my red scarf which is hanging around Mom's neck and stay there as she begins to talk. "Mrs. Campbell, this book was written by a known communist sympathizer, and therefore, it is anti-American. It's been pulled from the shelves in all respectable libraries in this country and overseas," she says, all puffed up and looking proud. And then, as if Mom isn't seeing her point, she hisses, "It's a dangerous book."

"How did you—where did you get this book?" Mom asks me.

"I—" but my answer won't come out fast enough.

"I pulled several dozen such subversive books from the shelves yesterday and put them aside. We are not entirely certain how they wound up on a rolling cart in the children's area." She pauses and looks hard at Mrs. Svenson, who up until now has been quietly rearranging pencils in a cup.

"People who read about communism support the people who write about communism, am I right? And people who defend communist propaganda—well, I would say their motivations are suspect, wouldn't you, Mrs. Svenson?"

Suspect? Is she saying I'm a suspect? Suspects run down alleys until they can't climb over the fence and then the cops slap the cuffs on them. Suspects sit under bare light bulbs and sweat it out until they spill their guts. Suspects wear black hats and stand and watch kids from sidewalks. I never thought of myself as a suspect. I didn't know that suspects read books.

Mrs. Pearson's acting like a kid on a playground pushing other kids around and trying to start a fight. I say nothing, and Mrs. Svenson says nothing, which is a good thing. But Mrs. Pearson has more to say.

"I'm sure we all agree that we have to be ever vigilant in our efforts to destroy the communist enemy that is creeping within and threatens to destroy our country. These writers are bad seeds,

Mrs. Campbell. Godless, bad seeds that we don't want planting evil ideas in the minds of our children. There are people who are working actively to destroy our way of life and enslave us to the Soviets. These authors have no place in our public libraries." Mrs. Pearson isn't leaving any room for argument in the conversation and reaches over to grab the dangerous book.

But Mom is faster.

"*1984* by George Orwell." She reads the title aloud. I have never seen my mother read anything other than her *Good Housekeeping* magazine, so I am kind of surprised when she says, "Orwell. I know this author. I read one of his books in college. And what's this other one?" She picks up the book that Bernadette had been reading, "*The Grapes of Wrath*?" she says. "I saw this movie. That's not dangerous. That's Henry Fonda."

"Filth," sniffs Mrs. Pearson.

I've heard Mom talk about Henry Fonda before. He's a movie star. Mom says he's a dreamboat. Obviously, Mrs. Pearson doesn't agree. Right now, it doesn't look like they agree on anything.

"*The Grapes of Wrath* was the 1940 winner of the Pulitzer Prize," Mrs. Svenson says softly. With her Swedish accent, it almost sounds like she's singing the words.

"Communists have been among us for a long time. Some people were communists when they arrived in this country." Mrs. Pearson says. She stares down at the top of Mrs. Svenson's head, whose eyes remain focused on the pencil cup.

Then Mrs. Pearson turns her attention back to Mom. "We can't let loyal Americans be deceived into supporting communists.

These books were pulled from circulation for good reason," Mrs. Pearson says, pronouncing every word carefully and precisely. No song in *her* voice.

"President Eisenhower does not support book banning or book burning," Mrs. Svenson says. It's hard to tell who's talking to who. The two librarians are both looking at Mom, but instead of talking to her, they seem to be talking to each other.

Mrs. Pearson stands, her spine a broomstick. "As a citizen and as head librarian, I take a strong stance against banning or burning books. I read the list of authors that Senator McCarthy listed as promoters of communist propaganda and I pulled their books from the shelf. I'm not banning books. I'm extracting dangerous authors."

"Excuse me?" Mom says, her head tilting to the side. "You're joking, right?"

"I don't joke about subversives, Mrs. Campbell. Steinbeck, Orwell, Thoreau, Hemingway, and that tramp, Dorothy Parker. They will not be turning our neighbors into puppets for the likes of Stalin, not on my watch."

"I'm glad to hear you don't believe in banning books and that you agree with the president." Mrs. Svenson speaks quietly, but she doesn't give in. "Because burning or destroying books, these are very dangerous practices. This is the work of the fascists, yes?"

"Are you implying that I am a fascist?" Mrs. Pearson's voice is a little higher, and she finally turns to look directly at Mrs. Svenson.

"Not at all." Mrs. Svenson smiles. "I knew it must be a simple mistake that those books were in the rubbish bin. This is why I put them back on the cart."

I think that Mrs. Pearson's face can't flame any redder, but it does. "It's not like I am burning the books, Mrs. Svenson. I would never, ever do such a thing as that. I am simply protecting the community."

Mom looks at them, and then I follow her eyes to the clock. It's five minutes after four. *Uh oh*, I'm thinking. They better decide on my prison term quick, or sparks are really going to fly. *Secret Storm* comes on at 4:15. You don't want to stand between Mom and a television set when it's time for her story to come on.

A bubble of silence expands to fill the space between us until Mom pops it. "I'll take them both."

"What?"

"Both of these books," Mom says. "I want to check them out. It's been way too long since I read a good book. I think I'll have to see what all the fuss is about."

"I'm afraid I can't let you do that. These books have been pulled from circulation," Mrs. Pearson says, reaching for the books. But Mom hands the books to Mrs. Svenson instead.

"You are in the book-lending business, am I right?" Mom stands tall and tries to stick a few stray hairs back in with a hairpin. It's hopeless, though. The hair falls right back down, and she tucks it behind her ear.

"Mrs. Campbell, as a mother I wouldn't think you would want to have such subversive literature in your house, let alone read it. You might want to have a conversation with that lovely

45

Mrs. Ferguson. You two are neighbors, I understand? Perhaps she could explain to you why these books have been pulled."

If I had a blanket, I would be pulling it over my head right now to protect myself from the fallout. Nobody compares my mom to Mrs. Fancy Pants in Pearls, which is one of the nicer names I've heard her call Bernadette's mom.

"It's a free country, last time I checked," Mom says, picking her pocketbook up off of the counter and plopping it back down again, just in case Mrs. Pearson missed her point.

And then with an *I gotcha* tone in her voice, Mrs. Pearson says, "May I see your library card?"

I know Mom doesn't have a library card. She doesn't need one; her *Good Housekeeping* magazine comes in the mail every Tuesday. So I guess this is going to be the end of it. Mrs. Pearson has my mom checked up against the wall and the clock's ticking down. Only, while neither one of them is looking, Mrs. Svenson scores.

"Why, that's no problem. We can get you a library card easily. I have the paperwork right here," says Mrs. Svenson.

And she does. She helps Mom fill out everything, and then Mrs. Pearson says Mom can't have a card until she brings in some identification. Then Mrs. Svenson says she'll vouch for her, and before you know it, we are standing outside the library in the cold. Mom struggles to pull her gloves on while holding the books, and I'm trying to figure out if I'm in the doghouse for being a thief and an instigator.

Mom pulls her coat together and throws the red scarf over

her shoulder like it's a feather boa instead of a hand-knit scarf made of crooked stitches.

"What time is it, Marjorie?"

"Oh, it's four-twenty, Mom. Maybe we can run home in time for the end of your story." I know she's worried that she's missing her show, and I turn toward home as fast as I can, but she catches me by the hood of my coat and stops me in my tracks.

"Good. Your dad and your sister won't be home for another half hour. I know it's only twenty degrees, but it feels like we need to stop by Stewart's Drugstore, don't you think?" she asks.

The ice-cream fountain at Stewart's is where Mom takes me for milkshakes when I have been good about going to the dentist or sitting still for a shot, or the time I caught poison ivy so bad I had to go to the emergency room. Or last summer when all my guppies died. And when our wiener dog, Schiltzie, went to live with a new family in the country. Every one of those times, Mom took me for a milkshake at Stewart's because, according to her, there's nothing like a milkshake to smooth out the rough spots.

"What do you say to that, my little instigator?"

"Okay," I answer. Who's going to say no to a milkshake? Even when it's twenty degrees.

We head toward Stewart's and I promise myself that the next time I'm allowed anywhere near a library, I'm going to look up the word *instigator*.

CHAPTER 5

"Students, I'd like you to meet your new classmate, Inga Scholtz. Inga has just moved here from Canada. Isn't that right, dear?" Mrs. Kirk says, smiling down at the top of Inga's head. And then to the rest of the class, "I know you will all join me in welcoming our new friend."

Mrs. Kirk stands with her arm around the new girl, who looks just like she stepped out of the pages of *Heidi*. Blond braids wind in two circles around her head. She's wearing an apron over her dress and heavy tan stockings that wrinkle around her ankles and the tops of some kind of little boot shoes that, for sure, I've never seen at the Buster Brown store where we buy our saddle shoes. On top of the whole outfit stretches a too-small aqua blue sweater gaping between the buttons because it won't quite reach all the way around her.

At first the new girl stands with one hand on her hip, but when she realizes we are all staring at her, she drops her arm and clasps both hands behind her back and lowers her eyes. I've seen this move before. As I try to remember where, I hear Mrs. Kirk calling me.

"Marjorie?"

That's my cue to come up to the front of the class and lead

the new girl back to my desk. My desk's just like all the others. A wooden box on four legs with an iron arm on one side that holds up the slanted desk part. One of us will have to sit sideways or tight against the iron bar to fit into the thing, and both of us will have to cram our books and papers underneath. The classroom's crowded and we won't be the only two kids sharing a desk, but I can't say I'm all that happy to no longer have a desk to myself.

I walk up the aisle and just motion her to follow me. She looks at Mrs. Kirk and then at me, and Mrs. Kirk nods. Once we return to my desk, there's one awkward moment when neither one of us knows who should sit first. I push the air with both hands, signaling her to slide in first. I figure since she's the newcomer, I have dibs on the outside seat.

As she bends to fold herself into the desk, I feel a tug on my skirt.

"Nice shoes," Mary Virginia whispers. Her whispering voice is loud enough to hear across a playground. I don't know whether to shush her or agree with her, but since Mrs. Kirk is giving me a look, I just sit.

Inga says exactly nothing for the rest of the day. She sits with her hands folded, being polite, but kind of just stuck in place.

We do our problems. Everyone except Inga, that is. Then we open to page 194 of our science books, where Inga pretends to read along about igneous rocks. Since that subject's about as exciting as, well, rocks, I don't think it's weird that she is only faking being interested. In fact, it makes me think I might even like her.

When we have to answer the questions at the end of the chapter about different kinds of rocks, she just watches me write and never unfolds her hands. I wonder how long Mrs. Kirk's going to let her slide along without doing anything.

After we return from lunch, Mrs. Kirk announces that the whole class is going to do something really fun. She's clapping her hands and trying to drum up some excitement in the room, but since it's afternoon, the only answer to her enthusiasm is the clanking radiator. Then she passes out some two-hundred-year-old books that have pictures of women dancing around with flowered crowns on their heads. As usual, there aren't enough books to go around, so everyone has to share. The ladies in the books are supposed to be from olden Greek times before people had to wear real clothes. In the pictures, the women are wearing drapey, see-through dresses that almost show their entire bodies. Mrs. Kirk wants us to turn to a poem on page twelve, but everyone seems to be stuck on the pages with the pictures.

The pictures have Owen Markey and Danny DiMario laughing so hard they snort. Mrs. Kirk wants us all to chime in together to read something called a Greek chorus, except it doesn't work because all the boys have caught the same snorting disease. Mrs. Kirk finally huffs, all disgusted, and snatches the books back. She directs us to sit quietly and think about our attitudes.

Instead, I think about how during our short attempt at choral reading, I noticed that Inga's lips moved, but there were no sounds coming out of her.

At afternoon recess, Mary Virginia pulls me by the coat sleeve until we're standing inside the monkey bars. She motions Piper Spencer over, too. Bernadette's out sick, or she'd be in on this conference, for sure. Probably leading it.

"What's she like?" Mary Virginia asks.

I shrug. I really don't know. Inga hasn't said anything.

"If that girl's from Canada, my mom's from Mars," says Mary Virginia.

"Did you see her shoes? She's right off the boat," Piper says, like she's sharing some secret we haven't all figured out already. "She has *old country* written all over her. Where do you think she's from?"

"I'm guessing Sweden or Denmark," Mary Virginia says, "Her hair's so blond it's practically white."

All the families I know come from somewhere else. Piper's family is Slovak. Mary Virginia's is Irish like Bernadette's, but they haven't been here as long. My family came over on the boat when ships still had sails, but both Piper and Mary Virginia have grandmothers who don't speak English. Being from somewhere else is pretty normal in our neighborhood.

Piper grabs both of our arms and leans forward. "What if she's German?"

German. The word hangs in the air like an insult looking for a place to land.

As sure as there are doughnuts every morning at Schwartz's bakery, there are plenty of Germans in this country, but as far as I can tell, they all landed here before the war. I hadn't heard of any new Germans around. Lots of new Hungarians and Polacks and lots of Jewish survivors, but no blond-haired Germans that I'd heard of.

"That would make her a you-know-what," Piper says.

"A what?" I ask.

"You know."

I shrug and throw my hands in the air. I have no idea what she's talking about.

"She's saying that you might be sharing your desk with a Nazi, you ding-a-ling," says Mary Virginia. "Does she smell like sausage?"

"She doesn't smell like anything," I say. They both look at me like I should tell them more, but there's not much to tell since the girl doesn't seem to talk. "Her sweater's kind of scratchy against my arm," I offer.

"She's homemade head to foot." Mary Virginia says, and she and Piper both nod. "I'll bet she's never even seen the inside of a department store."

"If I looked different like that, I'd just die," says Piper.

I don't say it out loud, but Piper does look different. She can't help it. She's almost as tall as Mrs. Kirk and has frizzy hair that her mother tries to control with clips and rubber bands, but it still pokes out in every direction. And Mary Virginia's different because of her loud voice and her bright, orange hair. She says her hair is not orange, it's red. But her hair's as orange as a tangerine. Every one of the O'Donnell kids looks like they fell off the same tangerine tree and then got dipped in a bucket of freckles. When they arrive at a school concert or PTA night, they light up the room.

But that doesn't stop them from staring at Inga, who's hugging her elbows and standing as close as she can to the school door. When the bell rings, she's the first one inside.

After recess, we all watch George Jacobi turn purple as he reads his book report off of index cards. When he gets the cards all mixed up and has to take a minute to sort them back out, Inga and I look at each other for the first time. I see that Inga's eyes are the color of the cloudless winter sky, pure blue.

I also see that she's scared to death.

CHAPTER  6

"Hey, Squirt!"

Frank.

I don't respond. Last time I checked, my name was not *Squirt*. I put my lunch pail in the sink and drop my schoolbooks on the desk in the kitchen. First thing I want after school is a snack, not an annoying big brother who isn't really my brother.

"Squirt, I heard you're banned from the library for being a pinko."

"Oh, gee. Guess you're wrong again, dumbhead. Mom fixed it and took both of those books out for me." Frank doesn't even have to try to be a pain. He's like a swarm of mosquitoes I just want to slap. I do my best to be cool around him and not let it show how he makes me itch all over.

"Yeah? Well, your dad took 'em right back this morning. Dropped them off at the library on his way to work."

"What?" And there it is. Frank gets to me. I pause and look at him hard. He can't be serious.

"You think you know everything. You just made that up."

"Nope. Check it out, babycakes. You think your dad's gonna put up with a red menace in the family? He'd lose his job, for one thing."

Dad would lose his job because of some books Mom checked out of the library? Me? A red menace? He can't be serious. I steam silently.

"You're so full of it." That makes no sense. Dad took the books back?

"Yeah? Well, maybe you conked out early last night and didn't hear the fireworks. Your mom's up to her neck in some kind of hot water and you're the one who put her there."

"You lie," I say. Only I say it a little softer because, come to think of it, maybe I did hear some yelling last night. I just figured they were yelling about money or Frank. Regular stuff.

But library books?

"What did you think? Your dad works at Chrysler. His job is top secret. Tanks and landing craft with gun mounts. The government don't take no chances with that. He had to sign the same loyalty oath my dad had to sign."

That's not all he signed, I think. But I don't say it out loud. Mom says I should feel sorry for Frank because he's a war orphan. Not the same kind of war orphans that Dad saw begging for food in Greece after the war, but a different kind of orphan.

Not everybody knows that Chrysler makes all kinds of war stuff like tanks and jeeps. They snapped my dad up after the war so he could give their real engineers advice about tanks. My dad was one of those guys in the war whose head stuck up out of the tank, and the real engineers are just eggheads who don't know their ears from their elbows when it comes to real combat.

Frank's dad used to have the same kind of job as my dad's.

Then one day, Frank's dad asked my dad to sign a paper promising to be a guardian to Frank if anything happened to him, since Frank's mom is MIA and his older brother's in jail. *MIA* means "missing in action," which basically means she disappeared.

Since Frank's dad had no one else to name in his will, Dad said he'd be Frank's guardian. Dad signed the paper on a Wednesday. The next Saturday night was when Frank's dad died. Not from natural causes. That's how Frank turned into an orphan and I got a big brother overnight.

So I know my dad signed that guardianship paper, but I've never heard of him signing anything else.

"Loyalty oath?" I make the mistake of asking out loud. This makes Frank smile. He's really got one over on me this time.

I hate that.

"Yeah. Your dad signed an oath saying he wouldn't do nothing to undermine the United States government."

"Wouldn't do *anything*," I say. Frank hates it when I correct his grammar. He glares.

I glare back. "That's just stupid. My dad is a war hero, why would he undertime the United States government?"

"That's *undermine*, little Miss Smarty Pants, not *undertime*. Look it up. And while you're at it, maybe you better yank your head out of your sandbox and listen to the news once in a while," Frank says. "You ever heard of the Un-American Activities Committee? Yeah, didn't think so. Well, they just found out that the army is crawling with commies. Crawling with them. So, everybody with a top secret job, they make them swear on their lives in writing that they are not a threat to America or gonna go out and sell secrets to the Russians. Bingo, bongo. See the connection?"

I don't see any connection at all. My dad would never sell secrets to the Russians. He's about the best American there is. "Liar," I whisper under my breath. But at the same time, I'm thinking maybe this loyalty oath thing is just dumb enough to be true, like the fact that liver tastes like skunk farts, but it's supposed to be good for you. I put on my liver face.

"True as I'm standing here. Teachers and librarians—them, too. They all have to sign. And don't you know that goes for tank designers just like your daddy, sweet cheeks. You checking out commie books you got no business reading could get your daddy fired and all of us out on the street. How would you like living in a refrigerator box under a bridge? You'd last about a week out there, using a curb for a pillow," Frank snorts.

"Oh, like you're so tough." I want to bang a chair over his head. I want to kick him where it hurts. Instead, I say, "I hear you cry sometimes, you know. I can hear you through the heat vents. Big tough guy."

Frank slaps a kitchen chair out of his way and lunges in my direction, but I am too fast for him and run to put the table between us. He tries to push the table aside just as Mom appears in the doorway.

"Stop right there, Frank." Her voice stops him in his tracks. He's breathing heavy and his eyes are on fire. He wouldn't dare make another move with Mom watching.

I feel a little smile starting until she turns to me, "And you watch your mouth, young lady."

We stop glaring at one another to look at Mom. Her eyes are red as Easter eggs and she hasn't put her lipstick on. "I don't need this from you two today." She squares the table back up with the chairs while we watch from opposite sides of the room. The anger swirling in the room slows. She takes a deep breath and stands up tall. She tucks some loose hair behind her ear. Then she puts both hands in the pockets of her apron and takes her lower lip in her teeth.

"I can't take this hatefulness." she says, her voice barely loud enough to hear. "No more. Not today."

Nobody says anything else. Frank and I turn in different directions so we can go back to ignoring each other. I grab a couple of graham crackers to take to my room. Frank jerks open the refrigerator and sticks his head in. Mom disappears into the living room to watch TV. I check the clock.

Almost 4:15.

CHAPTER 7

I stop in the hallway by the telephone bench, chewing on my graham cracker. I really want some peanut butter for my crackers and a glass of milk, but I'm not going back in the kitchen while Big Stupid is still in there.

I never really thought about Dad working on top secret defense stuff and it's hard to believe a couple of old library books might make him lose his job. I wonder if he carries secrets around in the car or in his lunch box. I stop munching on crackers.

What if that man in the black cap wasn't watching Bernadette and me at all? Could he have been looking to break into our house for top secrets? Was he a commie whose job it was to send pouches of information straight to the Kremlin? Was he trying to make us into puppets for Stalin?

I shake my head. That's silly. More likely, if anyone was casing the house, it was someone looking to rob us blind, not a Russian spy prowling for defense secrets to steal. Somehow this thought does not make me feel better.

I'm thinking I'll call Bernadette and see how she's feeling. Tell her about the new girl. Artie told me that she's down with a bad ear infection. Bernadette comes down with ear infections like the rest of the world goes to the grocery store. By that I mean on a pretty regular basis.

I pick up the black telephone receiver to dial her number, but I hear talking on the phone.

"Did somebody just pick up?" It's Mrs. Burke from down the block. I'd know her voice anywhere. It's smooth like syrup. You might think she's really sweet, unless she catches you putting one foot on her grass. Then it's war. She comes racing after you with a broom. This has happened to me and Artie and Bernadette maybe a hundred times. Bernadette and I used to think she was a witch because of the broom she likes to wave around and the fact that she keeps her curtains closed all the time. But it turns out she's just a secretary for Father Coughlin, the priest at Mary Virginia's church, the Shrine of the Little Flower. Dad calls it Shrine of the Silver Dollar. Dad says the priest she works for used to be on the radio and was on the side of the Nazis before the war. That makes her out to be a Nazi sympathizer in Dad's book, and he said we're allowed to walk all over her lawn anytime we feel like it. Mom says to steer clear.

We like to play next door to Mrs. Burke because Mrs. Papadopoulos sometimes surprises us with trays of yummy cookies with powdered sugar on top.

The first time Mrs. P. brought out cookies, it was a surprise. Now we're used to it, which is why their yard is our favorite place to play. Mr. and Mrs. Papadopoulos don't have any kids, but unlike Mrs. Burke, you can tell that they wish they did. For Halloween last year, they set up a long table with treats, and every ghost, vampire, Snow White, and Davy Crockett in the neighborhood dropped by for warm Vernors ginger ale, cinnamon sticks, and doughnuts.

"Hello?" Mrs. Burke says.

"Sorry," I say and hang up.

Bernadette's family has a private line, and even though Dad says that's an as-dumb-as-a-box-of-rocks way to waste two dollars a month, I wish we had one too.

Party phones might be okay in some places, but not if you wind up paired with people like Eugenia Burke. Mostly, I just wish Witch Burke wouldn't spend all her non-broom-swinging hours on the party line.

I sit on the telephone bench, breaking off small bits of cracker and trying to catch all the crumbs in my skirt. No books. No TV. No telephone. No going over to Bernadette's, since she's sick. I swing my feet back and forth, bored, bored, bored, until I notice the mail sitting at the bottom of the stairs.

A brown envelope.

I jump straight up, scattering cracker crumbs all over the floor. A brown envelope!

It's addressed to Miss Marjorie Campbell from the consulate of Brazil. And it's a thick one. I grab the envelope and fly up the stairs and slam the door to my room. From under my bed, I slide out the huge Hudson's Department Store box that's almost big enough to hold Carol Anne.

But now it holds the world. British Kenya. French Indochina. Spain. Sweden. Australia. Morocco. Brochures and maps sent to me *absolutely free* because I clipped a small advertisement from the back pages of *National Geographic*, taped it to a two-cent postcard with my return address, and sent it in.

I tear open the envelope from Brazil. This time it's not just a map. The package holds brochures, hotel information, three postcards, a message from Pan Am Airlines, and a map that opens as colorful and big as a beach towel. I trace the outline of the coast with my finger. The cover of the first brochure is a swirl of a dancer's red dress, with her face crowded into the upper left-hand corner. *Visit Brazil!* It says in tall white letters.

I do. Sitting on my bedroom floor I feel it throb with the stamping of the dancer's feet. I hear the clicking of castanets and the whip of her skirt. I forget about Frank and the returned library books. About Mrs. Burke and the new girl crammed into my desk at school. About Mom's sad eyes. Those are all just fuzzy chapters in a bad dream.

Brazil looks forward to welcoming me! There I will enjoy *endless sunny days,* no more ice crystals on the windows or frozen kneecaps. Instead, I can experience *glorious sun-filled days and magnificent moonlit nights, exploring more than four thousand miles of spectacular coastline where ocean breezes graze golden cliffs and sandy white* beaches.

Rio de Janeiro either is a festival or has one. At first I can't tell, but it has its own brochure, and I can read it to find out. I set it inside the box between the Eiffel Tower and the Pyramids for further study. Another brochure about cruising the Amazon claims I will see *majestic mountain peaks, caverns filled with sparkling crystals, and an untamed world of wildlife and waterfalls.* There are pictures I can crawl into. I feel the water spray on my face. Brazilians, I read, are *a hospitable, culturally diverse people who enjoy rich cuisine and lively music.* They value their families first, then education, and they lead rich spiritual lives. No mention of loyalty oaths or tight-jawed librarians with folded arms. No scary men in black caps just staring for no reason. Everyone in the pictures is smiling, looking as if they are having the best time ever.

From the manila envelope, a world of blue and green possibilities bursts into my world of dirty snow banks and crowded classrooms, and I fill my lungs with warm, moist air and soar like a parrot above the canopy of rain forest to rest on the highest treetop. I hear my name being called from below.

"Marjorie? Marjorie!"

I am sitting in a tree being tickled by green leaves when I realize, *yikes*, Mom really is calling me from below. From downstairs.

"Coming," I shout, as I jam the brochures into the coat box and slide it back under my bed. Her program must be over. Time to set the table.

"Coming!"

CHAPTER 8

As Inga and I settle in, I notice that she doesn't have any supplies. Not only are we sharing a desk, we will be sharing a science book, a reading book, a grammar book, a ruler—*my* ruler. I want to ask how we'll both be able to diagram sentences with only one ruler. I look at Mrs. Kirk for help, but she's busy telling Owen Markey and Danny DiMario that it's not okay to play bombs away with ice balls.

I dig through my pencil box and pass Inga a pencil I don't mind sharing. It's missing an eraser. She takes the pencil with a nod, but just like yesterday, she doesn't say a word. I point to the math problem on the board. That's Kirk's favorite way to start the day. She writes some word problem involving miles or apples or apples going miles, and we solve it while she takes attendance. Inga gives me that scared rabbit look again, and I stand up and retrieve a sheet of paper for her from the box on the corner of Mrs. Kirk's desk.

I can't believe I was even a little excited to meet this girl. She says nothing, and she knows nothing.

Inga folds her hands on the paper and sits like she's praying in church.

I'm not sure what "welcoming our new friend" means

exactly, but I'm pretty sure it does not mean I'm supposed to give her the answers to word problems. So I just do my work, and I'm done in about one minute.

Billy O'Brien leans over and asks, "You got the answer?" I sneak my paper over to the corner of my desk so he can see. If Billy O'Brien wanted my entire pencil box, notebook, coat, scarf, and boots, I would probably push them all his way, too. I know that's stupid, but that's the thing about Billy. He makes me feel stupid, even though I'm faster at word problems. He plays basketball. He's captain of the outside safety patrol and crosses kids at the corner of Coolidge and Catalpa, the busiest corner in the neighborhood. He delivers the *Free Press* to my house every morning. Dad reads it at the dining room table before I come downstairs in the morning. When I see it spread out there, I know that paper was touched by Billy, and it's like I just missed him stopping by.

Over Christmas break I set the alarm for 5:30 a.m. one morning so I could catch the paper when Billy threw it on the porch. I had a picture in my mind of how I would open the door and take the paper and smile, and he would really see me for the first time. We wouldn't have time to talk, but our eyes would connect, and after that, everything would be different.

I loved that dream. It glowed like a crackling campfire and made me warm inside.

But when Billy came by to fling the paper on the porch, we didn't connect at all. Instead, I hid behind the curtain.

Billy makes me do stupid things like that.

After I give the answer to Billy, I see him give it to Owen. Meanwhile, Inga is still just sitting there. We've been sitting hip to hip for a whole day plus thirty minutes and she hasn't said a single word. It's starting to get on my nerves.

I give her a little elbow, not hard. A nudge. I point again to the board. She looks at me and one tear pops out the corner of her eye. She wipes it away quickly. She looks at me like a squirrel does right before it dashes away.

And then I know. I don't know how, but I know. And I say, "English?"

And she lowers her head. Two more tears drop onto her paper.

I look at Mrs. Kirk, who's standing with her attendance book, asking if anyone knows why Bernadette isn't in school for the second day in a row.

"Earache," about eight kids shout in unison.

"Well, that girl needs a shot of penicillin so she can come back to class if she wants to pass this grading period." Kirk slaps her book on her desk.

"Who has the answer to this morning's problem?" She looks around at the raised hands and smiles.

"Billy. We know you have the answer. Enlighten us, young man."

And he does.

After the word problems we do round-robin reading, but luckily before it's my turn, it's time for recess. As soon as we hit the gym for indoor recess, I snatch Inga by the sleeve and pull her into a corner.

I don't have to say the words. She knows what I am asking before I can ask it. "Yah," she says, "I am speaking English. Just not so good to read."

Her accent isn't quite like Mrs. Svenson's. It's more like my swimming teacher's, Mrs. Edelstein's.

"I thought you were from Canada," I say. "I've been to Windsor, Ontario, and I know they speak English there."

The panicked, scared squirrel look returns and she turns away, but I grab her and turn her back. "Does Kirk know?"

Privately, Bernadette and I call our teacher Kirk the Jerk because she's kind of dense about things. But even the densest teacher in the world would know if a new girl couldn't read English. Wouldn't she?

"You help me? I read?" Inga blurts out the question in a half whisper, eyes darting around to see if anyone's listening.

"Oh, for cripes' sake."

"What is *cripe*?"

"Oh, never mind," I say. The fact is, *cripes* is my mother's favorite swear. What she uses for a swear word, anyway. There are worse words, but that's just what comes to me when Inga asks me to teach her to read English. How am I supposed to do that? But how can I tell her no? It's obvious she's desperate.

"Yes, mind," she says. Urgent. Like learning the word *cripes* has a deadline and she's missed it.

"Don't you worry about learning that word," I say. How do you explain a bad word to someone who hasn't even learned the good words yet?

"What is *chew*?" she asks.

"*Chew?*" I repeat.

"Yah," she says. "Don't *chew* worry. What is *chew?*"

I bust out laughing. Inga looks at me, and for the first time, she halfway smiles.

"*Chew* is funny word?" she says. "You teach me *chew?*"

"I'll teach you *chew*," I say, still laughing.

"When?"

This girl is something else. "I don't know, how about tomorrow?"

She nods. "Tomorrow and the next tomorrow."

"The next tomorrow?" I ask. "You mean the day after tomorrow?"

"Yes!" She nods, all excited. "The tomorrow after tomorrow and the tomorrow after that, even."

This girl makes me laugh. Not laugh at her in a mean way. She's like a walking *National Geographic* magazine, strange and fascinating, and I can't wait to turn the next page.

The bell rings. Time to go back to class. I head for the door, and it's Inga's turn to catch me by the sleeve.

"You teach me *cripes*, too," she says. She doesn't wait for an answer as we both join the flock of kids flowing into the hallway.

CHAPTER  9

"You tree. Dare. Stay dare. Later for you."

Mrs. Edelstein flaps her arm at the side of the pool, indicating we should take a seat on the edge. Three of us sit down at the spot where she pointed, feet dangling into the deep end. Me, Ben Zielinski, and Tony DeMarchi. We are hugging our arms and shivering. The non-swimmers.

Learning to swim at the YMCA is the worst way of all to learn. I don't care if the Y is closer than the lake. In a lake you can wade in a little at a time. You can hang on to an inner tube and float, pretending you can swim. The sun warms your back. You can fake it and still have a good time.

I used to love that kind of swimming at the lake. It didn't matter to me that I couldn't really swim, and Mom didn't seem to know the difference. But then Andrea Soboleski's cousin caught polio at Cass Lake, and now he's in an iron lung, and I'm stuck with swimming lessons at the YMCA, where the frost grows on the windows so thick you can't see the sun, and the chlorine makes my eyes burn. I tug at the strap on my bathing cap and wait. My kneecaps quiver. I watch Mrs. Edelstein coach the other kids through swimming widths across the deep end. She's wearing a whistle around her neck and a gold bracelet on the same arm as her tattoo.

I remember the first time I saw a woman with a five-digit number tattooed on her arm like Mrs. Edelstein. It was Mrs. Schwartz from the bakery. We were in the locker room here at the Y, after a family swim night last fall. That was the night Mom caught on that I couldn't really swim and signed me up for lessons.

I'd never seen Mrs. Schwartz's bare arms before, and I asked her why she had a price tag on her arm. Mom threw a towel over my head.

"Oh, Mrs. Schwartz, I'm so sorry," she said. "I apologize for her. She doesn't . . . I'm so sorry."

"No harm," said Mrs. Schwartz.

I pulled the towel down, and Mom put it right back.

"I'm just so, so sorry."

I was having trouble breathing. I pulled the wet towel off again. I didn't understand. Why did she have numbers on her arm? Why was Mom apologizing? Why wasn't I ever allowed to ask any questions? Mom wedged herself between Mrs. Schwartz and me, hiding me like I was embarrassing her.

Mrs. Schwartz patted Mom on the arm. "Enough, already. No worry."

Then she bent down to where I was peeping out from behind Mom's elbow and looked me in the eye. "One day, my darlink." She touched my face. "One day."

Lucky I never said anything like that to Mrs. Edelstein. She doesn't have time for questions or to look kids in the eyes. She's the type who steps on your fingers if you won't let go of the side of the pool.

After I said that price tag thing to Mrs. Schwartz in the locker room, Mom made Daddy explain to me about the Nazi concentration camps. I sat on a footstool in the living room, and Dad sat on the very edge of his chair and told me how his tank knocked down the wall of one camp and they found all these Jewish people in there. They were like skeletons just wandering around. He said the GIs knew the Nazis had put people into prison camps. "But we weren't prepared for that," he said, almost whispering. He wasn't looking at me, he was looking at a place far away.

"Were you scared?" I asked. He shook his head.

"You fed the people, right?"

Dad didn't answer me right away. He bit his lip. For a few seconds, he closed his eyes. Just when I thought he might be done talking, he went on. I could tell he was pulling the words from deep inside. He told me that the soldiers starting passing out their K rations, but it made the starving people sick. Some of the people even died because they'd been hungry for so long, their stomachs couldn't handle food.

"They died?" I asked. This was the worst thing I'd ever heard. It made my heart hurt and my eyes burn. "You tried to help them, and they died?"

"We didn't know." Dad lowered his eyes.

Then he told me how the nurses who traveled by bus arrived and told the GIs to switch and start the people in the camp out on chewing gum and soup that was hardly more than hot water.

I wanted to know what kind of bus? And why did the Nazis

lock up all the Jewish people? Where did the people sleep in the concentration camp? How did they find their way home again? But Daddy just looked at me and shook his head. "Later, kid, when you're older. That's it." He slapped both knees, stood up, and went outside to wash the car.

With grown-ups like Dad and Mrs. Schwartz telling me that I would find out what happened in the war later, when I'm older, it made me wonder if I wanted later to come. But then later came—this year, sixth grade, when Mrs. Kirk showed us a newsreel about the concentration camps. And after seeing the pictures of bunks and ovens and barbed wire, I can't forget them. They're printed in black and white in my mind. And when those pictures flash though my memory, I smell chlorine. Just like the locker room at the YMCA.

Finally, Mrs. Edelstein turns to the three of us. Ben, Tony, and I practice *reach and pull* in the air while sitting on the side of the deep end. We practice like crazy, tipping our heads from side to side. Mrs. Edelstein goes over to the wall and grabs her long bamboo pole.

"Okay, you tree. Girl first," she yells. I slip in the water and cling to the side of the pool like a baby hugs its mother's leg. This is my second round of beginner swimming lessons. I know the routine. What I haven't figured out is how to swim across the pool. When I see Mrs. Edelstein pick up her bamboo pole and start to walk toward my fingers, I take a deep breath and let go.

I forget *reach and pull* because I am too busy with *splash and gasp*—trying not to drown.

"Kick!" Mrs. Edelstein yells.

I do. I kick like there are pythons at the bottom of the pool. I kick and splash as fast as I can, until I start to choke and my legs won't work anymore. I can't breathe. Just when I know I'm about to die, I see the bamboo pole and grab hold.

I hug my freezing arms, sit on the side of the pool, and shiver through Ben and Tony's splashing. Both of them finally make it across the pool without grabbing for the bamboo pole. As soon as I hear the whistle, I dash to the locker room, Mrs. Edelstein yelling after me, "No run, no run."

Mrs. Edelstein comes into the locker room after class to talk to Mom. Mom's sitting on a bench with her winter coat in her lap. I'm struggling to pull clothes over my ice-cold legs with shivery hands.

"This girl?" She points at me. "Too tin. She sink." She picks up my arm and holds it out for Mom to check, then drops it. "Cannot teach." She throws her other hand up and waves it back and forth like she's trying to erase me from where I am standing.

Mom forces a fake smile. "Marjorie is quite healthy, thank you."

"She's not have enough meat on her bones to float. You feed her good and take classes in summer." Mrs. Edelstein nods. "At city pool. You take her dare." She turns, and exits, leaving me still standing with one leg in my corduroy pants and my arm hanging where she dropped it. Mom's mouth gapes open. The fluorescent bulb frizzles overhead.

"Sorry," I say to Mom after Mrs. Edelstein's gone, the swinging locker room door swishing behind her.

"Just get dressed, honey," Mom says. "It's all right."

But it's not. I've just been kicked out of the library and swimming lessons in the same week.

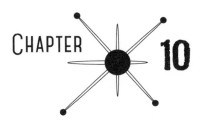

CHAPTER 10

After school, I meet up with Carol Anne in the crush of kids in the front lobby. I wave at Artie and pass him a folder of homework for Bernadette, who's still home with her earache. I see Inga talking to her mom. She comes every day to pick Inga up. Carol Anne immediately starts to pull me toward the door, but I pull back.

It seems natural to ask Inga if her mom would let her come over after school. Inga bounces on her toes as she turns to ask her mother.

"Go wait there." I point Carol Anne to a not-so-busy area by the door. She goes over and leans her head against a window, making faces at the kids outside waiting for rides.

Inga's mom stands in the lobby of the school, gripping her coat around her like it's trying to fly away. Her face is surrounded by a black wool scarf stretched over her head in a triangle and tied tightly under her chin. Underneath, her hair is pulled back in a bun. Inga has to translate my invitation to her, and I can see that her mom is worried. Inga may not be able to read or speak English that well, but it's obvious that her mother doesn't speak a word of it.

"Stupid DP!" someone shouts as a group of boys knocks into

Mrs. Scholtz as they rush for the door. Mrs. Scholtz catches her balance, grabbing Inga's shoulder.

"Go back home."

"Get out!"

"Nobody wants you here."

Insults explode around us as the boys push through the front doors. I stick out both arms and try to protect Inga and her mom.

"Shut up!" I hear myself yell.

Inga attaches herself to her mother.

"Over here," I point to a place by the wall where we can stand and talk without being mowed down. And then I yell in the direction of the boys, "Stupid . . . stupids."

I don't know what to call them. Not one of those boys could frighten me on his own, but they seem scary as a group. Even to me. Inga's mom's hands are trembling, her fingers covering her mouth.

George Jacobi sticks his head back in the door and yells, "DP, go home." I can hear the other boys laughing on the outside stairs. I take a step toward the door, and bellow, "SHUT UP!" at the top of my lungs. They all take off like a flock of squawking pigeons.

"DP" stands for a *displaced person*, someone who lost their home in the war and came over on the boat to start a new life. Mom says I shouldn't call anyone a DP in case they might take it the wrong way. Dad says it's not like calling an Italian a *dago* or an Irish person a *mick*. That kind of talk can get you punched in the nose, or at least pushed over on the playground. There's no meanness attached to the term *DP*, according to Dad.

"Don't pay any attention to those dumbheads." I say, wanting to take the hurt look out of Inga's eyes. She may not know perfect English, but she knows *get out*. And she must have heard the term *DP* before.

In my neighborhood we have DPs from Greece, Ireland, Russia, Italy, Hungary, Poland, Slovakia, and now wherever Inga's family really came from.

Mrs. Scholtz pulls a hankie out of her coat pocket to wipe her eyes as Inga guides her to the side wall, taking small steps. DP may not necessarily be a mean thing to call someone, but there was no mistaking the meanness in how those boys had pushed Inga's mom. It sure punched the breath out of me.

I stand facing Mrs. Scholtz. She looks small and lost.

I'm pretty sure what Dad would call Inga's mom. He'd call her a German. I continue to wait and watch as Inga talks to her mom in hushed words I can't understand.

Meskcovic. Jablonski. DeMarchi. O'Brien. Papadopoulos. I can think of plenty of houses in our neighborhood where the families speak another language at home. Mrs. Kovacs, the Hungarian woman who comes and helps Mom wash floors the right way—on your hands and knees—only speaks about four words of English. Mom says it doesn't matter because Mrs. Kovacs knows how to speak the language of cleaning like nobody's business.

Her grandson, who comes to the door to walk her home, is as American as me. I never met her son, but he probably talks in broken English like a DP. That's how it goes with people who come to this country. Some things get passed down—like how

77

Mary Virginia's orange hair and freckles were passed down from her mom—and some get passed *up*.

Speaking English? That's something that gets passed up. Little kids who came here as babies or were born here, they teach English to their parents and grandparents, the ones who came here in the first place. It takes having kids for DPs to catch up with talking American.

A three-year-old could tell that Inga and her mom aren't from here. Their shoes, coats, the confused looks on their faces. As much as I like reading about other countries and dream about visiting them, I can't imagine what it would be like to be a DP in some country where you don't know the language or how to dress. I wonder if I would change my name to fit in better, like how Henry Finklestein's dad changed their last name to Eaton when they started going to the Episcopalian church. Or how Milinko changed his own name to Mike. For sure I would change my shoes if they laced up to my ankles like Inga's.

As Inga and her mom whisper, I recognize two words that sound like *nine* and *yah*. When they finally settle on *yah*, I write my phone number and address on a piece of notebook paper and give it to Inga's mom. Mrs. Scholtz also makes me write down my father's name and Stewart's Drugstore, the place where we will meet up at 5 p.m.

I grab hold of Carol Anne just as Mrs. Scholtz takes Inga's mittened hand in her red, scratched-up one. I try not to notice as we all walk out of school together. Holding my mom's hand in front of the whole world is something I outgrew as soon as I started school. All I have ever heard about Germans is that they are mean and dangerous. That doesn't seem to fit Inga and her mom.

At the corner of Coolidge and Catalpa Road we stop and wait for Billy to tell us when we can cross. Billy wears his gold safety patrol captain's belt and stands with his hands out, holding us back from the curb. I stare at my shoes and telegraph mental signals to make Mrs. Scholtz let go of Inga's hand, but instead she bends and grabs mine, too. I'm already holding Carol Anne's hand. We look like we are about to crack the whip. Billy waits, checks the traffic both ways, and then steps to the side to let us pass. I quickly pull away from Mrs. Scholtz, but not before Billy sees.

"Hey," he says. A single word from Billy is enough to make my tongue knot up and my legs turn to stone. Inga and her mom start to cross. Inga looks over her shoulder at me just in time to see that I'm stopped and my face is on fire. She smiles.

"Go," Billy says and points to the crosswalk. I hurry across, pulling Carol Anne like a wagon.

"That boy, you like?" asks Inga when we reach the curb on the other side of the street.

"Let's go," I don't even pause to say good-bye to Mrs. Scholtz as I turn my burning face towards home. For someone who doesn't speak English, Inga sure understands a lot.

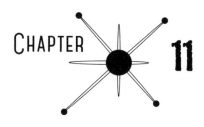

CHAPTER 11

Inga and I make a quick stop in the kitchen when we arrive at my house. I explain my favorite snack, and together we spread peanut butter on graham crackers and quickly make a break for my room just as Frank comes in.

"Hurry," I say.

"Who is?" she whispers as I push her up the stairs.

"He's not my brother, but he thinks he can boss me around anyway," I say. Inga looks confused. "He just lives here." Frank's too hard to explain to someone who barely speaks English.

And Inga would be way too hard to explain to Frank.

Frank hates Germans.

I use my hip to slam my door closed and immediately start to study my bookshelf for a book to begin Inga's reading lessons. Does she like horses? But *Black Beauty* might be kind of hard for a beginner. *Little House in the Big Woods*? That's easier, but what does a German girl know about prairies? There's always Nancy Drew. *The Secret of the Old Clock*? While I'm trying to make up my mind, she wanders over to Carol Anne's shelf of picture books.

"*Georges le petit curieux! J'adore ce livre!*" she squeals.

"You talk French?" I ask her, surprised.

"Oui! Ce livre, c'est mon préféré." She's hugging the book, and even though I don't understand French, it's not hard to tell that she loves *Curious George*.

"You speak French *and* German?"

"Oui." Inga nods. "But I come here from Canada," she insists. "Yah?" She waits for me to agree.

"Sure," I say.

The sun coming through the window makes Inga's braids practically glow. I wonder how this German girl bounced to Canada and then to Homer Elementary School. All I have ever heard about the non-Jewish kind of Germans is that they are Nazis and the worst people who ever lived on the planet. Watching Inga flip through *Curious George*, I decide there must be different kinds of Germans: the Nazi kind and the Inga kind.

Inga bounces with excitement. She studies each page like it's a scrapbook of favorite memories. Then she passes it to me. "You read in English?"

Curious George, Inga, me, and the man with the yellow hat. I read a line and she repeats it, pointing to each word. Sometimes she beats me to the punch and says the line first in French. But we still read every word in English.

After we finish, I pull *Curious George Rides a Bike* from the shelf. Grandma Mona gave it to Carol Anne for Christmas. Inga's never seen this one. She strokes the cover of the book like it's a pet cat. She nudges me to read it all the way through. When the monkey gets his job back at the animal show, riding around in circles with his stupid little bugle, Inga's enjoyment runs through

81

me. My fingers tingle as I turn the pages. My voice is breathless, as if I'm reading an action adventure instead of a baby book.

The book is new to both of us since I don't make a habit of sitting around reading Carol Anne's books. Inga studies every drawing as I read. When I finish, she motions me to go back to the beginning. We sit reading *Curious George* until the sun's no longer coming through the window. I glance up at the clock and jump straight in the air.

"Hurry!" I slap the book closed. We tear downstairs to pile on coats and mittens and grab our hats. We make it to Stewart's Drugstore just in time. Inga's mom is waiting outside on the corner. She spots us and takes a bare hand out of her pocket to wave.

We come up to her, and she reaches out to stroke one of Inga's braids. Both of us are holding our hats in our hands. Inga's mom makes a *tick tick* sound with her tongue. Inga flops her hat on her head. Mrs. Scholtz then tips her head at me and raises her eyebrows.

I smile at her. She stares back.

"Hut." Inga taps her head. And then she corrects herself. "Hat."

"Oh!" I pull my hat down snug. "Okay?"

Mrs. Scholtz nods. I guess it doesn't matter what country you come from, moms seem to speak the same language when it comes to their kids' ears hanging out bare-naked in the cold. I watch them walk away, hand-in-hand.

That's when I start to worry. What will I tell Bernadette

about Inga? For sure I can't tell Mary Virginia that Inga can't read. She'd announce it to the world and make her feel bad.

And then there's Frank. Did he hear us talking? Did he hear Inga's accent? Will we have to hear his whole rant again at dinner about how *the only good German is a dead German*? What will Dad say?

I turn towards home and jam my hands in my pockets, holding my worries in two closed fists.

CHAPTER 12

"I'm not eating it." I clamp my mouth shut tight as a bear trap.

"Just a taste."

"I tasted it before." I hate liver and onions. I hate liver and onions more than beestings. Liver lasts longer, and it's sickening. When there's a liver smell in the house, I try not to breathe. Mom and I are in a war over liver. She tries chopping it up and sneaking it into the mashed potatoes. She tries scrambling it with eggs. Mom says liver creates red blood cells and that it builds strong bones. Just the word *liver* makes me gag.

"It—smells—so—bad," I choke.

"Keep an open mind and taste it. You don't know until you taste it."

Holding my throat, I beg, "Please, Mom. I really can't."

"Let her go, Lila. She's putting me off my feed here," Dad says. He gives me a little wink and I gaze at him with gratitude pouring from my eyes.

"Her swimming teacher thinks we aren't feeding her well enough and that's why she can't swim," Mom explains.

"Don't suppose liver's gonna turn her into Esther Williams, Lila."

Esther Williams was not only a swimmer, she was also a

water ballet expert. I have seen her in old movies on TV. She just smiles her way along in the water, swimming on her back with one leg sticking up. I nod my head off. Nasty liver is never going to turn me into a movie star or make me dance in the water at the YMCA.

"Calf's liver is very high in iron," Mom says. There's a hint of that pathetic tone in her voice, and I know I've won.

"Double vegetables," Mom orders, which seems like a good deal to me even if my choice is soggy lima beans. Anything's better than liver.

Frank clears his throat like he's about to make an announcement. "So, Marjorie. You want to tell your dad about your little Kraut friend that you had over after school?"

Dad, Mom, and Frank all stare at me. Even Carol Anne stops piling her mashed potatoes into the shape of the Empire State Building. "What?" she asks, shrinking in her chair before sliding to the floor and under the table. Carol Anne may be only a kid, but she can smell an argument like I can sniff out liver.

"Inga? Oh, she's from Canada," I say, cheery as Minnie Mouse. I reach for more lima beans like they're chocolate cake and I can't wait to dig in.

"Yeah. And I'm from China," Frank snorts. He leans toward Dad and whispers, "Kraut."

I turn to Mom. "You always told me if there was a new kid at school I should be friends with them, right?"

Mom nods, watching me take two heaping spoons of limas.

"Well, Inga's a new kid, and it just so happens, Mr. You-

Think-You-Know-Everything, she moved here from Canada." I pop some beans in my mouth, my eyes returning Frank's mean stare. "And for your information, she speaks French."

"What's the girl's name, again?" Dad asks.

"Inga."

"Inga what?"

"Inga Scholtz," I answer quietly.

"What'd I tell ya," Frank says. "Kid's right off the boat. Old fashioned dress, ugly shoes. Got that Hitler-Youth look, blond braids and all."

The dining room is quiet, no forks clinking on plates. No one lifts a glass.

Frank says to me. "I know a DP when I see one. I heard you two talking. She's German."

Mom starts. "Well, I'm sure she's a nice little girl."

"Nice kid of some nice little Nazi, no doubt. The Canucks opened the floodgates, and now look at what we have here. Not only Nazis in the neighborhood, but a Nazi right under your roof." Frank's all kinds of mad, and I can tell he wants Dad to be mad, too, since Daddy fought the Nazis just like Frank's pop did. Only Dad isn't mad. He just folds his napkin beside his plate and stands up from the table.

In the silence that he leaves behind, we hear the back door shut. Dad's gone to the garage where he keeps a little heater so he can work on his car even in the winter. Not the car we drive around in, but an old clunker that doesn't run. One day he's going to buy a new body for it, but in the meantime, it still needs a lot of work.

"So, that's it?" Frank says, his hands flying up in the air.

"This Inga—she's just a child, Frank," Mom says, stacking plates in front of her and brushing scraps onto a saucer with her knife. "And we really have no idea who her father is or was." Then she lifts the cloth and says, "Come out of there, Carol Anne."

"Inga's really nice, Mom. Honest. She likes *Curious George*. Her dad can't be a Nazi."

"Germans was all Nazis. Wasn't any man over there not in the war 'less he was blind or too damned dumb to carry a gun. They got down to where they was drafting kids." Frank's fired up, looking back and forth between Mom and me to make sure we're watching.

"Were," Mother says quietly. She uses her feet to search out Carol Anne.

"What?" Frank barks.

"They *were* drafting kids," Mom corrects him. "But you shouldn't go making up stories in your head about this girl's father without knowing who he is or where he came from."

"I don't have to be making up stories, Mrs. Campbell. I'm living the story. Me. Right here." Frank stands, and *crash*, his chair dumps over behind him. He doesn't reach for it or even stop to notice. Carol Anne magically appears in Mom's lap like she's been drawn out of a hat.

"Look at me. I got no family left. Nazis turned my mom against my dad and she took off. Nazis killed my pop same as if they pulled the trigger. And you go and invite some Nazi kid over to the house. You're lucky I didn't throw her out. Just like that." Frank snaps his fingers.

"Frank." Mom's voice thumps like a gavel. "Sit." And then to Carol Anne, "Go play, sweetheart." She sets her down and nudges her gently toward the doorway.

Frank clumps his chair back up and slams himself into it. He's fuming. I watch him like I'm watching a house on fire and there's nothing I can do.

"You don't remember before the war," Frank says to me. "But I remember. I remember when my pop was a person." Frank leans his face into his hands with his elbows on the table. Mom doesn't tell him not to.

When he raises his head from his hands, his eyes are shiny, blinking. "My pop, he taught me to ride a bike. He took me to see Santa Claus. He was one person before the war and a different person after. Now he's dead, and it's all because of the Nazis." Frank's cheeks and his nose and his eyeballs are all red and growing redder. He's so close to exploding, I hold my breath and wait for the bang.

Mom reaches to touch his arm, but he jerks it back.

"Frank, dear. It's war that did that to your pop. We don't know what he saw." Mom's voice comes out warm as hot chocolate with marshmallows on top. Frank sits with his arms crossed, holding his anger tight.

Mom just keeps on talking. "We can't know what pain your pop carried home. I saw the same thing happen to my Uncle Ned after the First World War. Soldiers can be hurt in places you can't see. Even Jack." Mom hesitates. "I know he doesn't talk about it much, but the war is with him every single day. Not just his trench mouth or the bullet wounds or the injuries to his feet. Those are the things he jokes about. It's what comes back to him in his dreams. Sometimes those wounds are the hardest to heal."

"Yeah, well what about my wounds? What about how my brother's sitting in a prison cell? What about how my pop chased off my ma and I don't know where she is? What about how my pop's dead and I still have to get up every day like it means something? What about that? And you!" His eyes flash like lightning looking for a place to strike and then land on me. "What about you inviting the enemy right into the house?"

The back door opens, Dad calls out, "Frank, you come out here and give me a hand?"

Frank's bolts up from his chair and stands at attention. Not moving.

"Frank?" Dad's voice nudges him one more time.

Frank stomps toward the garage. The door slams so hard the pictures jump on the walls.

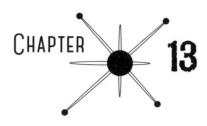

CHAPTER 13

Mom's washing, I'm drying, and Carol Anne is making the forks dance into the drawer.

"Come on, Carol Anne. This isn't playtime." Mom swooshes plates through the water faster than usual. She checks the clock and says, "Oh, my word. It's almost seven o'clock." She checks out the front window. "My ride will be here any minute."

"What ride?" I want to know.

"Mrs. Papa—" is all she that has a chance to come out of her mouth before Carol Anne cranks up her siren scream. She does this every time Mom goes past the mailbox. Whether she's headed to the grocery, the drugstore, or bridge club, Mom always leaves with an earful of screaming.

"Shh, shh, Carol Anne." Mom pulls Carol Anne's face into her apron as she nervously glances at the door to the garage. Then she kneels down. "Shh, sweetie. Mommy's going to a meeting. Your sister'll help you into your pajamas, and she'll even read you a story, won't you, Marjorie." This doesn't sound like a question the way she says it, so I don't give it an answer.

I cross my arms.

"What kind of meeting?" I want to know.

"Just a meeting," Mom says. "I was all set to tell everyone at dinner, but then Frank became all upset and, well, here we are."

"Where are we?" She's not going to weasel out of answering me this time. "What kind of meeting?"

Mom stops for a minute, thinking. Then she says, "It's a planning meeting, um, about the bridge club."

I've never heard of a planning meeting about bridge club before. Bridge club happens every other Tuesday, when Mom's friends in the neighborhood get together to play cards. The ladies in the bridge club take turns having it at their houses. No planning meetings involved. When Mom entertains the bridge club, it's the only time other than Halloween that candy comes in the house. Mom and Mrs. Kovacs clean for days until the whole house smells like lemon oil and Spic and Span. Carol Anne and I collect butter-mint bribes to not touch *anything*.

Carol Anne's gearing up for another scream, when Mom claps a hand over her mouth. "Don't ask so many questions, Marjorie. I need your help tonight." And then to Carol Anne whose eyes are bulging like basketballs, she says, "How about a nice bath? With bubbles."

"Bubbles as tall as the Empire State Building?" *Sniff, sniff.* Carol Anne's been stuck on that thing ever since we watched the King Kong movie on TV. She likes to build it up and dive-bomb it with imaginary airplanes.

"You bet. I'll start the water for you right now."

Of course that means she's going to start the water, dunk Carol Anne, then dash out the front door when Mrs. Papadopoulos pulls up front in her dumpy Nash Rambler Deliveryman station wagon with the Greektown Pizza sign on the side. Mom's pulled this trick on Carol Anne a hundred times and she never sees it coming. Leaving Carol Anne is like ripping off a Band-Aid, better if it happens fast and when she's not looking.

Mom streaks up and down the stairs, grabs her pocketbook and is almost out the door when I call to her.

"What do I tell Dad?"

One thing about my dad is, he doesn't like surprises. There's no chance one of us would ever hide behind a door and then jump out and yell "surprise" at my dad. He always sits with his back to the wall so no one can sneak up on him when he's not looking. One time when the phone rang right next to him, he turned the telephone table over and threw a chair. It broke the front window.

"Don't let your sister drown up there, and tell your dad Lydia picked me up for bridge."

"But it's not Tuesday."

"Bye. Back in a couple hours," Mom says, closing the front door behind her.

"Mom?" Carol Anne pokes her bubbly head out of the bathroom doorway. I hustle her back in the tub and in two seconds she's giggling and swishing around in the bubbles. It's kind of amazing how quickly she gets over it after Mom actually leaves. I watch as she makes soap circles on the tile, and wonder why Mom is acting so mysterious.

I rub a place on the steamy window so I can check out the corner where I saw the man in the black hat. Nothing. But that doesn't mean there's nothing to worry about. He could be back tomorrow. And there's Inga to worry about. And all of Frank's angry questions about her. And now Mom, disappearing into the night.

Dad's always telling me I have to be battle ready, but how can I do that when I don't know who the enemy is? Mom said that she's met the enemy and it's Mrs. Pearson at the library. The Nazis are Frank's enemy. Dad used to be enemies with the Nazis, but now he's signed a loyalty oath, so now is he just enemies with commies? And then there's a strange man in the neighborhood who just stands and stares. When I add it all up in my head, it's like I'm sinking in a pool of enemies, and there's no Mrs. Edelstein holding out a bamboo pole to save me.

Pretty soon it's lights out and Carol Anne and I are both in bed. I'm dozing off when Dad appears in the doorway to ask if I know where Mom is. I don't even lift my head from the pillow to mumble that she's at a bridge club meeting.

I'm sunk in a deep sleep when I first notice the yelling.

"How can you think this is okay? You know how I feel, right? I made myself perfectly clear? Are you hard of hearing?" Dad's work boots walk the wood floor. "So tell me, what goes through your brain that you think you can go behind my back?"

Mom's voice is like background music at Hudson's department store—I can barely make it out. Dad's voice is a marching band with tubas and drums.

"Did you think I wouldn't catch you? Do you think I'm stupid? I'm away for six years and you stay here playing college girl, and now you think you're smarter than me?" I hear a slam. "And then you lie to your own daughter. You're a liar, Lila. Plain and simple."

Mom's voice again. A soft humming. No words I can understand.

"You just won't be satisfied until you get me fired, will you? Let me explain this to you again. George Papadopoulos owns a pizza joint. He has his own business. I work for Chrysler Defense Engineering. Defense, Lila. The spotlight's on me more than on him, but he better watch himself, too. I can't afford for you to put me in a position where I have to be on guard against those boneheads looking into un-American activities. I don't care if they burn books. I don't care if they burn down the whole damned library. I'm the guy who goes to work every day to pay the house note so my family doesn't wind up on the street."

"It's just not right," Mom says.

"I'll tell you what's not right. You making me look like we're going commie. You didn't pay any dues to those Friends of the Library did you? 'Cause that's what they'll look for. *Are you or any member of your family a dues-paying member of any subversive organization.* That's what they'll ask me. Simple choice, Lila."

Mom's crying now, her muffled words sobbing out in little bursts.

Dad's voice rises and falls as he paces back and forth. "The list of banned books was made so's they could get red-leaning books out of the Army libraries. Local libraries are just following recommendations from Congress. Congress, Lila. You and the

Friends of the Library gonna stand up to Congress? You got something up in your high hat the United States Army don't?"

Doesn't. I think to myself. Only I know Mom's not about to correct Dad's grammar at this point. Not when he's making the windows rattle.

Mom's voice. Then the squeak of the bedsprings. I picture my dad sitting down next to Mom. The argument quiets, but Dad's words are impossible not to hear.

"Your heart's in the right place, Lila, but your priorities, they're are all wrong. See what I mean?" The bedsprings squeak again, and I can hear Dad's boots plunk one at a time onto the bedroom floor.

"Look at all those rich guys in Hollywood," he continues. "Blacklisted. Communist sympathizers. Actors, directors, writers. Millionaires and they couldn't even buy their way out of it. Didn't matter if there was proof or not. Someone just accused them of sympathizing and they were out of a job.

"Remember the Rosenbergs? Ethel went down same as her spying husband. Did you see how Congress is dragging Army brass up for questioning? The Army, Lila. McCarthy and his crowd think the State Department, the Supreme Court and the whole Army are infested with communists. Lila, those meathead red baiters ain't just fooling around. You see how it reflects on me if you're a sympathizer with the library?"

I know the word infested. We had a dead elm tree in the yard that was infested with big black carpenter ants. When Dad sawed into it, the ants poured out like an oily waterfall. Dad grabbed the hose and drowned the ones left in the tree, but tons escaped and headed out in single file to go infest other trees. Some of them made it into the house, which drove Mom crazy out of her mind. So Dad sent us all to the movies and sprayed the whole house with DDT. The DDT killed most of the ants, but it also killed all of Carol Anne's goldfish. From what I've seen, infestations are more contagious than chicken pox and hard to stop once they are set loose.

Is the man in the black hat part of an infestation? Is he looking for a new place to invade? Is he just a scout with thousands more behind him?

What kind of DDT do you use on communists?

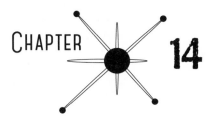

CHAPTER 14

Friday morning at school, I take a good look at Inga. Her wool stockings, her Heidi dress, and her too-tight sweater buttoned up to the neck. She smiles as soon as she sees me and rushes over to our desk and slides in. It isn't just her face that's smiling either. She's smiling with her whole self.

I shrink back, a little afraid she's going to give me a hug or something embarrassing. I look to see if Mary Virginia is watching. I'm not sure how she would take it if she knew about Inga coming over yesterday.

I think about how hurt Inga would be if she had heard Frank calling her a Nazi.

Truth is, if Bernadette hadn't been out with an earache, I never would have invited Inga over in the first place. There never would have been a fight with Frank. What if Frank had actually said something to her about being German? Knowing Frank, he sure wouldn't have said it in a nice way. Come to think of it, there's not a chance I can ever have Inga over after school again. First, because of Frank and second, because of Bernadette.

Having Bernadette as a best friend is lucky for me because no one would want her as an enemy. Frank's a loudmouth and likes to pick fights, but Bernadette is meaner. She can be mean in ways no one else can see except the person she's being mean to. Bernadette has a way of taking up a lot of space in any room she's in. People notice her, and they pay attention to what she says and who she likes and doesn't like. I'm pretty sure she wouldn't be so excited about me making friends with a girl whose stockings droop in folds around her ankles and whose braids hang practically down to her waist.

Bernadette isn't going to be sick with an earache forever.

"Good morning, Marjorie," Inga sings. She puts a small square wrapped in waxed paper down on the desk in front of me. I just stare at it. Inga gives me a nudge with her elbow. "For you," she whispers.

"Thanks," I say and slide the square under my desk.

"Taste!" says Inga, still all smiles. "Lemon bars. Mama make. Very good." She licks her lips in case I'm not getting what she says.

"Shh," I say. "Here comes Kirk."

Mrs. Kirk continues to stand in the hallway waiting for the tardy bell. I stare at the blackboard. Inga stares at me.

Being friendly is like pouring Carol Anne's bubble flakes into a bath. Once the flakes mix with the water there's no way you can turn them back into flakes again. Being friendly for even one day changes things. People expect that you will be friendly forever. I realize then it's not going to work out being friends with Inga. I also know it isn't going to be easy putting the flakes back in the box.

I sit there trying to hold myself apart from her, even though it's pretty much impossible since we have to share a one-person desk. I take out a pencil and paper and get busy on the word problem on the board. This time I don't retrieve a piece of paper for Inga from Kirk's desk. She taps my arm. I let her out of the desk without looking her in the eyes, and she walks up and takes one for herself, but it stays blank because I don't read the problem to her.

I turn to see if Billy needs the answer, but the question's too easy.

I feel like I'm in a box.

It's not that Inga isn't nice. She is. She's so nice. It's not her fault. I just should have thought it through before I asked her over and made friends with her. Like Dad told Mom. I need to keep my priorities straight.

Being friends with Inga might be okay with Bernadette out sick, but what's going to happen the next time Bernadette wants to stop for doughnuts after school? Who am I going to trade Nancy Drew books with? Am I going to be stuck reading *Curious George* for the rest of my life? Besides, what good is it making friends with someone you can't even ask over to your house?

If Bernadette hadn't had a stupid ear infection, none of this would have happened, and I'd still be sharing my desk with a stranger. My head swirls. I am so angry. Angry at me. Angry at Bernadette and her stupid ears. Angry at Frank. But mostly I'm angry with Inga.

Why me? Why couldn't Kirk have put her with Piper or

Mary Virginia? Why am I the one who has to know that she can't read English? Why am I stuck feeling sorry for her? What if her father really *is* a Nazi? Or was a Nazi? Or can you ever stop being a Nazi once you are one?

I sit there convinced that I am never going to speak to Inga again. Not ever.

By recess I'm alone and Inga's alone and I can barely stand not talking to her anymore. When the bell rings to go back to class, I walk up to her and say, "Hi." Her eyebrows seem a little surprised, but she doesn't say anything. We walk back into class kind of beside each other.

After lunch I eat the lemon bar while Inga watches my face like it's a scoreboard. When I smile, she claps like a home run just went up on my forehead. I keep smiling and she smiles. I show her how to use my ruler to make perfect lines for diagramming sentences. And then I tell her what the words are and why some of them go on straight lines and some on slanted lines. Kirk comes by and asks how we are doing. "Just fine, Mrs. Kirk," I say.

"Excellent," she says, satisfied.

Inga whispers, "Thanks you."

"It's *he thanks, I thank*," I whisper back. Inga looks confused. She points at Mike. "He thanks?"

"No, *I thank*."

"You welcome." She smiles.

"Oh, never mind. Just put your name on the top of your paper." It's too hard to not be friends with Inga with us sharing the same desk. Bernadette will just have to understand. Inga and

100

I can be friends at school, but Bernadette will still be my best friend at home. I don't know what to do about recess, but I figure I can deal with that on Monday.

After school when Inga asks me to come over on Saturday, I only hesitate for a second before I say okay. What's the big deal, anyway? Bernadette's mom isn't going to let me come over to her house and she's not going to be allowed outside. I promise to bring some books with me and that I will come over as long as my mom agrees. I'm laying promises out all over the place as Inga writes her address on a scrap of paper. She only lives a couple of blocks from my house. I ask her to write down her phone number so my mom can call and talk to her mom, which is the only way I'm going to be allowed to visit.

But it turns out that Inga's family doesn't have a phone at all, not even a party line. My mom's not going to like that; she likes a phone number in case of emergencies. Inga looks worried, but I make another promise and tell her that I can make my mom understand.

Mom understands as long as she can drop me off and meet Inga's mom and make plans to pick me up in four hours.

On Saturday, when we ring the bell, Inga translates so my mom can talk to her mom. Mostly they smile and nod, and then the door closes and I gulp down a whiff of Inga's house. It does not smell like sausage.

CHAPTER 15

Inga's house is hollow. Even though I leave my snow boots by the front door, my stocking feet echo when I walk across the bare wooden floor in the living room. In the kitchen there's a table and three mismatched chairs. Stockings, shirts, and two nightgowns hang on a clothes tree by the kitchen sink. Mrs. Scholtz has one side of the sink full of soapy water and the other side with rinse water. There's not a dish in sight.

Mrs. Scholtz is washing clothes in the kitchen sink. Not just her silky things like slips and nylon stockings, but men's work pants and shirts. I've never seen this before, and try not to look at the sink. But my eyes become stuck there.

"I didn't know you could do that," I mumble.

"What?" Inga asks, leaning toward me.

I end up staring and trying to make sense out of Mrs. Scholtz washing work pants in the kitchen sink instead of in a washing machine. I figure it must be a German thing that they haven't gotten over yet.

Even though the kitchen isn't quite as empty as the living room, the walls have no pictures and the floor has no rug. Mrs. Scholtz speaks softly to Inga, who shakes her head and reaches into the cabinet and pulls out an unopened package of graham crackers and a jar of peanut butter. When she unscrews the top, I can see it's a brand new jar, the peanut butter lying in a perfect swirl.

We spread our crackers in silence. Mrs. Scholtz watches with her hands in the pockets of her apron. She has that same worried look on her face she wore the last time I met her. She pulls a hankie out of her pocket and quickly wipes both eyes. I wonder what's in her head that she can't say because she doesn't know English. I wonder what makes her cry.

Inga's room is not completely empty. There's a single bed with sheets and a blue blanket pulled up neatly to the edge of a smoothed out pillow. No bedspread. But that's not all. No bedside table and no lamp. No clock or shelves with books, games, and puzzles falling out on the floor. No pile of stuffed animals in the corner. No dresser, no mirror.

I look in the closet where three dresses hang. One, two, three. And number three's all white and obviously too small for sixth-grade Inga. It was probably the first communion dress worn by second-grade Inga. No corduroys. No jeans. No spring raincoat hanging around waiting for the weather to warm. Maybe the most amazing thing about the closet is that the floor inside of it glistens like a mirror.

"Wow," I say. In my whole life, I have never seen a totally empty, polished closet floor. This is stranger to me than the work pants in the kitchen sink.

Inga looks at me. She's wearing her mother's worried face. The face she made when the boys at school called her a DP.

"Your closet's so . . . clean." Inga peeks around the closet door to look where I am looking. I want to ask, "Where's all your stuff?" But I stop myself.

My closet's overflowing with stuff. Belts and hats. Stray mittens. Doll clothes and dress-ups. A piled-high box of Grandma Mona's old jewelry. Pull toys Carol Anne outgrew six inches ago. I don't remember not having stuff, though I don't suppose I was born with stuff. Stuff just gets collected as you go along. Stuff is stuff. Up until today, I have always just taken stuff for granted. It never occurred to me that some people don't have stuff.

Any thoughts I have about helping Inga look a little less like a DP and more like an American so that she can fit in better at school disappear when I take a look at her closet. We spend the rest of our time together looking at the books I brought and reading them aloud.

I read first and then Inga reads to me. Once in a while I have to explain a word, but mostly Inga knows the meaning of words when she hears them out loud. She follows along with her finger as I read, and then her finger retraces the words as she reads. I've borrowed books from Carol Anne's shelf, books with lots of pictures and just a few words. I also put a Nancy Drew in the stack. For a girl who already knows two languages, it won't be long before she is ready for books without pictures.

From inside one of the books I pull out a folded map of Canada. It's from my National Geographic collection. We open it and Inga points out Montreal and says that's where she used to live.

I believe her. I believe Inga moved to Detroit from Canada. I don't ask her how long she lived there, though. Was it a year? A month? A day and a half?

Instead of talking about her clothes, I help brush her braids into a ponytail. We go and look in the mirror in the bathroom. Her hair's too heavy to pull her ponytail up high where it belongs, but even so, she looks more American without the braids. Not much, but it's a start.

We wander back out to the living room. Two chairs. No sofa. No television.

"Who's that?" I ask, pointing to two framed pictures on the mantel.

"Oh," Inga says as she taps at her heart with her hand. "This one my grandpapa and grandmama. This one my family: mama, papa, brother, me." Inga is only about three years old in the picture, and her brother looks to be a couple years taller.

"You have a brother?" I ask.

She shakes her head and looks away.

"You don't have a brother?"

Inga touches the boy's face in the picture. "My brother, he goes to heaven with grandmama and grandpapa," she explains. One hand lingers on the face in the picture, the other hand she holds tight on her chest as if her heart might run away.

"Your brother died?" I ask. As soon as I say it, I want to slap my hand over my mouth. What a brainless thing to say. Except what *can* I say? All I have ever known are girls who complain about having brothers. Big brothers, little brothers, doesn't matter.

In my experience, brothers are the most annoying people ever invented. I've never known anyone who had a brother who was happy about it. But I never met anyone who had a brother who died, either. "I'm sorry," I say.

She nods, eyes trying to hold in tears. She's still holding her chest with her hand.

Just then, there's a soft knock at the front door. It's Mom, who normally just honks when she comes to pick me up at a friend's, her signal that I should shake a leg and run to her car. This time, though, Mom stands inside the front door trying to tuck the loose hair behind her ear while Inga goes to find her mom.

"No English," I whisper at Mom as I pass her the books and spin into my coat.

Bam. That's when I see it. Hanging on a hook on the wall.

A black cap with a button on top. It's more than a little worn, with loose threads on the brim. My mouth falls open as I stare.

Inga catches me with my eyes glued to the black hat and says, "Next time you meet my papa. Yes?" She smiles, hands clasped behind her back.

In her posture I see the dark shape of a man wearing a jacket zipped up to the neck. I picture how he stood, the wind whipping his pant legs. How he pulled his hands behind him.

Inga's father is the man in the black cap?

I am frozen in place. I close my mouth and swallow. When Inga reaches out, smiling, to pass me my hat and mittens, I respond like a robot. I have questions. But it's no time to be starting a conversation. It's time for good-byes.

Behind me, my mom is welcoming Mrs. Scholtz to the neighborhood and telling her if there's anything she can do, please just let her know. Mom says, "I'd be happy to show you around, if you'd like. You know, on Eleven Mile Road there's a butcher shop where you can buy homemade kielbasa sausages." Mom's talking a mile a minute, "Oh, I know kielbasa doesn't come from Germany, it comes from Poland, but they are practically right next door. Poland and Germany, I mean. In the same ballpark, as we say. But you don't know about ballparks yet. Do you? Well, you'll know soon enough." Mom smiles like she's actually having a conversation with Inga's mom.

"Mom." I stop her. She's just going overboard, trying to be friendly, but not a word of what she's saying does Mrs. Scholtz understand. I widen my eyes at Inga who whispers, "I tell her. Is okay." Inga and I may not have grown up speaking the same language, but when it comes to talking about moms, we don't need words.

But what about dads? Does her dad joke around and make up stories? Does he cheer for the Red Wings? He looked so scary when I saw him watching Bernadette, Artie, and me, back when I thought he was a spy.

I try to remember why I thought the man in the black hat was so scary in the first place. Maybe I thought he had to be a villain because he was wearing a black hat. The bad cowboys on *The Gene Autry Show* always wear black hats, so it makes sense that spies would wear black hats. Or does it? Maybe it was the way he just stood and stared at us. Maybe I was just scared of him because he was a stranger.

I can feel the questions bubbling up inside of me. Does Inga's dad wipe his mouth with the back of his hand instead of his napkin when he eats? Does that drive Mrs. Scholtz crazy like it does Mom? Does he laugh at his own jokes? I couldn't see his face that day. Does he have a laughing face like Mr. Papadopoulos?

My head spins and I am practically dizzy enough to fall on my face as I bend to pull my boots on, teetering on one foot, then the other. I have to grab the wall so I don't fall flat. I see that Mrs. Scholtz is nodding at Mom—and smiling. Not a broad smile, just the imitation of a smile. Still, it's the first time she hasn't looked worried.

"Here," Mom says. She hands the stack of books to Inga. Big colorful picture books topped off with *The Secret of the Old Clock*. A mystery book for a mystery girl.

"Just keep them as long as you like. There're more where those came from," Mom offers. Inga nods and hugs the books. A few more awkward words and handshakes and we are finally out the door.

In the car, Mom looks at me as she starts the engine. When I still haven't said anything by the time she reaches the corner, she asks, "So?" I don't answer at first, because I'm not sure what to say.

"Earth calling, Marjorie. You there?"

"Umm, I think. No, I don't think so. I don't know. I mean, I need to figure something out," I stumble in my head as I gaze out the window for answers to the questions that I didn't ask.

"Can I help?" Mom has one eye on the traffic light and the other on me.

Help me unravel the stories I'd made up in my head about the man in the black cap? Help me understand that he wasn't a commie or a spy, that he wasn't casing the house to rob us blind or steal defense secrets from my dad? Help me figure out if the man in the black cap is just Mr. Scholtz, Inga's papa? Or the neighborhood Nazi.

"I'm thinking I need to loan Inga some knee socks. You know. To help her fit in at school," I say, because I know I have to say something to my mom or she will stop the car and plunge my brain like a stopped-up toilet.

"Lend, not loan," Mom corrects. "I would say that Scholtz family needs some furniture before they start worrying about what's fashionable."

I look out the window at the lumpy snow piles flashing by. What Mom doesn't understand is Bernadette and how she's going to pitch a royal fit over those saggy wool stockings if Inga keeps wearing them every day. Mom only knows the smiling, "How's your husband?" side of Bernadette. If Mom had the whole picture, she might realize that some things are more important than chairs and lamps.

I sigh big and loud so she knows that I don't agree with her.

"Don't give me your Sarah Bernhardt routine, Marjorie. I'm already on edge today and I don't need it."

Sarah Bernhardt is an actress who went out of style about a hundred years ago, which just goes to show how out of touch my mother really is.

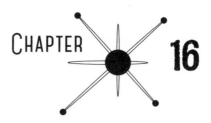

CHAPTER 16

Mom pulls into the driveway, but instead of immediately popping out of the car, she turns off the engine and just sits with her hands on the steering wheel. We sit for a long minute.

"I need you to do something for me, Marjorie." She turns and claps her gloved fingertips softly. "It's going to be fun. Just like Nancy Drew."

"Nancy Drew?"

"Yes," she whispers, her voice all bubbly with fake excitement. "And you are going to be Nancy."

"Yeah, right, Mom. What is it?" I cut her a side-glance and stare straight forward. She's treating me like I'm four years old and about to be vaccinated—she doesn't want me to scream, so she promises me that she'll take me to Stewart's for a milkshake when it's all over. The thing is, I know her tricks, and when she talks like this, it just makes the four-year-old in me want to scream even louder.

"Really, Marjorie. This is very important and . . ." she looks at the closed garage door, "a deep, dark secret."

"Cut it out, Mom. I know you're trying to bribe me into doing something. I'm not Carol Anne. You want me to open the garage?" I start to open the car door.

"No!" she screeches and leans across me to lock the door. "No," she repeats, a little more calmly. "No," she says a third time, with a sigh. "I guess you are too old for me to fool you."

"I guess so, Mom," I stare up at the roof of the car. "Just tell me what you want me to do."

She lets a lot of air out and kind of hums, or moans, it's hard to tell. She shakes her head and tucks her hair back. She's stalling. I cross my arms.

"I need you to go inside very quietly and then come back and tell me exactly where your dad is, if he's working in the garage or asleep in his chair. Can you do that for me?"

I smile. "Oh, I get it. You went shopping. What'd you buy? New shoes?"

We've pulled this sneak act before. The last time involved red high heels. She sneaks new clothes into the house, and then when Dad asks her, "Are those new?" she says, "Oh, my word. I've had these for years."

"Kind of," she says. "I have a box in the trunk. All I need to know is if I have a straight shot from the front door to the stairs."

"What kind of box?"

"A box. That's all. I don't want to leave it in the trunk of your dad's car, and you don't need to know everything."

I don't answer, and I don't move.

"It's just a box. Mrs. Papadopoulos asked me to store something for her, and I told her I would. That's all."

Only I know that's not all. If it were just a box she'd be taking it in through the garage door like she does the groceries. She'd ask Dad or Frank to carry it in the house for her. She certainly wouldn't need me to go in the front door to scout out where Dad is.

"Sounds fishy." I cross my arms.

"Marjorie Elizabeth, I don't need you to give me any grief. I'm in enough trouble already. Just take yourself in that house and do what I asked you to do. Now get while the getting's good, or we'll both be in hot water."

If I'm going to be boiled in hot water with Mom, I'd like to know what for. I reach over my shoulder to unlock the door and jerk on the door handle harder than I need to. She reaches over and touches my arm. "Better check to make sure Frank's in the basement, too," she says, and then she holds her finger to her lips. "Shh."

I open the front door quietly and quickly check out the living room. Carol Anne is playing alone with a mess of doll stuff all over the floor. No Dad and no Frank. No sign of them in the kitchen or dining room either. I go to the front door to signal the all clear to Mom. She jumps from the car, clicking the door closed silently, and darts around to the trunk. I see the trunk lid open and close, and then she bumps around the side of the car, teetering under the weight of a heavy cardboard box. She plunks her feet down hard, and her head's tilted back, her neck straining. It's a very heavy box.

"Hold the door," she hisses as she steps onto the porch. She comes in and I watch her boots climb the stairs and turn into my room. I ease the front door closed and follow her up the stairs.

"Shut the door!" she huffs as I enter my bedroom. The box sits on my bed. "Lock the door."

"I'm not allowed to lock the bedroom door," I say. The last time Carol Anne locked the bedroom door, Dad had to climb a ladder and break the window to open it again, but not before she'd used Mom's *Love That Red* lipstick to draw on the mirror, the wall, the door, and herself. The time she locked herself in the bathroom, she licked the top of the toilet cleanser can before Dad could break in. So we don't lock doors in this house. That's the rule.

"Move it!" I do as Mom asks as she looks around the room, sizing it up. "Now, I need a place to put this."

I flip the lock on the door, shaking my head. "We are going to be in so much trouble." I'm not sure why I think we're headed for trouble, but I can just feel it.

Mom throws her coat over a pile of Carol Anne's stuffed animals, leaving one hand on the box at all times. It's like there are alligators inside the box and she doesn't want them to escape.

"That's the deep, dark secret?" I walk toward it sniffing the air.

"Look, Marjorie. If I tell you something, will you promise not to tell anyone?"

"Sure," I say. I really want to look in that box. It could be Ancient Greek art that Mrs. Papadopoulos smuggled into the country. It could be pictures of naked Ancient Greek women draped in see-through dresses like the ladies in Kirk's books. It could be buried treasure. It could, in fact, be an alligator. I have no idea what's in the box, and it's making my fingers twitch wanting to look.

"I'm serious, sweetie." Her voice softens. "You can't tell anyone. Not Bernadette. Not your dad. Not Carol Anne. No one."

"Okay, okay," I say, stretching to look under the flaps of the box. I'd probably promise her the moon in a bowl if she let me look in the mystery box.

"You think there might be room under your bed for this?" She sinks down on her knees and looks under the bed. I see my opportunity and flip back the top for a look.

"It's just books," I say, disappointed. Books? That's the big deal? "Mrs. Papadopoulos wants us to store some old books for her?"

Before Mom can even answer, we hear Carol Anne trying the door. "Mommy?"

"Just a minute," Mom answers, but not before Carol Anne starts to pound. "Mommy! Mommy! Mommy!" She cries, louder, louder, louder.

Mom pulls out my National Geographic box from under the bed and motions me to help her lift down the book box. "Hold your horses, sweetheart," she yells at Carol Anne.

"Hurry," she whispers to me.

We struggle the box onto the floor and slide it under my bed, way up against the wall. The door vibrates as Carol Anne starts kicking. "MOMMY! MOMMY!" We hear heavy steps on the stairs followed by Dad's voice, "Lila, you in there?" He tries the door.

"I'm here with Marjorie, Jack. Give us a minute."

"The door's locked. Why's the door locked? There are no locked doors in this house."

"I told you," I mouth to Mom.

Mom stands up on her knees. "We're having a little girl talk, can you give us a minute?"

"What'd you say?" he yells. Carol Anne's screaming is like a river that doesn't stop.

"G i r l   t a l k." Mom stretches out the words real long, as if Dad doesn't speak English.

"Oh. Okay, then. Girl talk. Carol Anne, you come with me." I hear his feet clomping down the stairs, Carol Anne's screams disappearing into the distance. Mom and I sit on the floor in the kind of silence that's left after a train's gone through.

"This is almost too much." Mom grabs her forehead with her fingertips, thinking hard. "Let's slide your map box back under the bed."

We do.

"It's okay, Mom. Nobody ever goes under there, not even Mrs. Kovacs." Mom looks like she needs convincing. "Really. I won't tell anyone, but just so you know, this makes zero sense. Hiding a box of Mrs. Papadopoulos's old books? Why?"

Mom leans against the bed. "They aren't her books, exactly. They're kind of library books. Or books that used to be in the library, anyway. And now they're . . ." she hesitates, thinking, "on a little vacation. Under your bed with all your travel brochures. Kind of fitting, no?"

I pull the bed skirt down and smooth my covers. "All hidden. Can't see a thing."

"You can't tell anyone about this, Marjorie."

"Yeah, I know. If I tell, we'll have to live in a cardboard box under some bridge."

She puts her hand on my arm. "If you say one word, there's no telling what would happen. The police could come. It would be bad. Really bad. Do you understand? Mommy could go to jail."

"Jail?" I seize up inside.

"Don't look so alarmed, my sweetheart. Mommy's really doing a good thing, it's just your dad might not see it that way."

"Or the police?"

"Well, yes. Or the police." She stands and picks up her coat from where she flung it on the stuffed animals. A teddy bear stares straight at me and I feel the crazy urge to turn him toward the wall so he can't see what we're doing.

"We need to end this girl talk and go join the family before Carol Anne explodes," Mom starts toward the door.

"That's my girl talk?" I ask.

Actually, I've already had the girl talk. Bernadette has two older sisters and they've told me everything I need to know. Being twelve does not mean I'm stupid.

I have also read just about every Nancy Drew book there is. I know what hiding a box of illegal books under my bed makes me. It makes me an accomplice.

Mom smiles. "We'll have that girl talk. Not today, though, okay?"

After we unlock the door and go downstairs, the rest of the evening settles in like a typical Saturday night. We eat and watch *Beat the Clock* and *The Jackie Gleason Show* just like the rest of the world. Then Carol Anne and I turn in so Dad can watch *The Saturday Night Fights*.

I slip under my covers thinking about Inga's hollow house and the box of books under my bed. I wonder if her dad watches the fights. I wonder how her brother died. I wonder if heaven's a real place and if Tommy Fisher might meet Inga's brother up there, or if there are boundary lines around countries in heaven like there are here on earth. Does everyone speak the same language in heaven? What if that language isn't English?

Thoughts swirl until my mind's so clouded I have no choice but to fall asleep. But not for long.

CHAPTER 17

Bing bong.

The doorbell?

Bing bong. Bing bong. I check the clock. 12:30 a.m.

Lights on in the hallway. Dad's feet on the stairs. The front door opens. I see Mom's bathrobe flip by my open bedroom door as she runs down the stairs.

My heart turns into a fireball. I sit up straight in bed and don't blink.

The cops have figured out where the books are already?

Someone must have seen us unloading the box from the car! I imagine Mom being taken away in handcuffs in her pink bathrobe and wonder if they will let her at least put on her boots. My ears are ringing and I pant heavily through my nose, my mouth clamped shut. This is it. The end of the world isn't coming in the form of an H-bomb; it's coming as a knock on the door in the middle of the night. I think about throwing the books out the window, but I'm too scared to move.

"George," Dad says as the door squeaks open. "Come on in."

Mr. Papadopoulos? Not the police? I don't breathe, waiting to hear more.

Why would Mr. P. be here? At first I'm relieved because no one's less scary than Mr. Papadopoulos, who sings when he brings you a pizza and never runs out of laughter. I take a relieved breath, but then it hits me. I sit straight up in bed.

"No!" My voice escapes into the dark room. I look over to see if Carol Anne is awake, but she's sprawled out on her belly fast asleep. She kicks at the covers and rolls over.

"We're doomed," I moan. There could only be one reason for Mr. P. to come to the door at this hour. He must have found out about Mom and Mrs. P. and the books and now they're both in hot water.

But hot water is a lot less scary than jail. I'm still scared, but not too scared to move. I pop out of bed and tiptoe to my doorway.

Mr. Papadopoulos stamps the snow off of his feet. Voices mumble from downstairs.

Maybe he's just here to warn us that the cops are on their way. Maybe there's still time.

Quick! I think. I have to hide the evidence. My eyes pierce the shadows of my room, looking for options. Where could I hide a box of books? Can I lift it by myself? I run to the window and give it a tug. Frozen solid. If I could break the window, I could throw the books down one at a time. But that makes no sense; the house is probably surrounded. I need to cover for Mom so she can slide out the back door under the cloak of darkness. I dive halfway under my bed and pull out my map box. Before I can imagine the next scene in the movie screen of my brain, I hear Mr. P.'s booming voice announce, "I'm going to be a papa!"

A papa? I sit up on my knees, listening hard.

"We got the call. The girl has reached her time. We have to be in Charleston, West Virginia, by morning."

"Let me put on some coffee," Mom says.

"No, no. No time. My friend, I need three hundred dollars to pay the hospital bill before they will give us the baby. The banks are closed."

Dad whistles. "Good God, George. I don't keep that kind of money in the house."

"Yes. Yes. I know. Whatever you have. I write it down here and pay you back after the banks open Monday. First thing. Anderson give me fifty, Fred DiMario, forty-three. I'm going up and down the street. I'm coming close, only need sixty-three more."

"Let me see what's in my tea can," Mom says, and I hear her running into the kitchen.

"I've maybe seven or eight bucks in my pants upstairs." Dad bolts up the stairs. I hear change falling on the hardwood floor and then he's in my doorway.

"Daddy?" I whisper. "What's Mr. P. doing here in the middle of the night?"

"He needs to borrow some money, baby. You still have that five bucks that Grandma Mona gave you in your Christmas package?"

"Sure." I reach into my bedside drawer and pull out my Annie Oakley wallet with its one, lone five-dollar bill. He doesn't wait for me to pull out the bill. He just snatches it up and dashes out my door and back down the stairs.

"That makes twenty-seven bucks, George. I wish it was more."

As Mr. P. walks back out onto the porch, Dad asks, "Is it a boy or girl?"

"Is a baby! Opa!" Mr. P.'s voice booms in the night.

"Opa!" my dad calls back as he closes the door.

Crouched at the top of the stairs, I can feel the rush of cold air on my bare feet when Dad closes the door. The lock clicks and Mom starts up the stairs.

"Let's go to bed, sweetie. It's late."

"Is Mr. Papadopoulos in trouble?" I ask.

"Not at all!" says Mom, smiling. "They're having a baby tonight."

"I didn't think Mrs. P. could have babies," I say.

"This baby's coming special delivery. Now, back to bed."

I may not know everything, but I know that babies do not come in a box, special delivery. "What?" I ask.

"They bought a baby from West Virginia," says Dad. "Tell her plain and simple, Lila, and then that's it. I don't want to be up answering questions for the rest of the night." Dad disappears into their room.

To know my dad is to know that *that's it* means no more questions. But telling me plain and simple isn't enough, so I whisper my leftover questions at Mom as she follows me into my room.

"How much does a baby cost?" I ask as Mom tucks the covers around me. "Why did they have to go to West Virginia?

Do they have baby stores there? With real babies?"

"They hire a lawyer to do the buying, honey. I don't exactly know how it works, but I know it's done. And the baby will have a loving and welcoming home, that's the most important thing."

"But how much?" I want to ask if some babies cost more than others or if they give discounts if you buy more than one, like two-for-one sales on cereal, but I don't push my luck.

"Oh, I think Lydia said it costs about five hundred dollars, if you count in the hospital bills, now go back to sleep."

After Mom leaves my room, I pull myself up to look out the window. The Winslows' porch light is on. I can see the outline of Mr. Papadopoulos in the open doorway.

I fall back on my pillow and think about a baby being born somewhere in West Virginia. I even consider pulling out my map box from under the bed and using a ruler to measure how far away it is and how long they will have to drive. But with Dad home, it's too risky for me to be poking around under my bed since my map box isn't the only thing under there.

I stare into the darkness, looking for answers. Carol Anne kicks her legs again in the next bed. Even though I can't see her, I know she's pulling her stuffed dog close. She missed everything, which is typical. I wonder if Mom and Dad would have paid five hundred dollars for me or for her. They pretty much got us for free. Five hundred dollars is a lot of money. But when you think about it, it's less than most cars cost, and babies last longer.

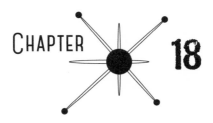

CHAPTER 18

I've never had a secret from Bernadette before. I've known her since we had our picture taken in our underpants, standing beside her wading pool with goofy grins on our faces and our bellies hanging out. We weren't even two years old. Someday when Mom's not looking, I'm going to take that picture down from its place on the side of the refrigerator and set it on fire.

This is Bernadette's first time outdoors in over a week. She's wearing earmuffs, a scarf over her head, and a hood over the entire business. Her head looks so big it's like she has a globe sitting on her shoulders.

I wonder as I watch her approach if she'll be able to see the secret on my face. I can't even tell her that there's something I can't tell her, because I know she could weasel it out of me. Luckily, she has other news and starts talking as soon as she sees me.

"It's the best," Bernadette says, describing her new 45-RPM record player. "It has one of those thick stems, so you don't have to put plugs in the records, and you can stack up eleven records in the changer."

"You have eleven records?" I can't believe it. A week ago she didn't even have a record player.

"Nah. Mom only gave me four records, the McGuire Sisters, Rosemary Clooney, Pat Boone, and Perry Como. "This Old House" isn't bad, but the rest of the records are dullsville. I still have my Christmas money, and my sister said she'd walk me to the record store one night after school. They have little booths so that you can listen to the record before you buy it."

"Your birthday's not until June." I point out the obvious.

"I know. But Daddy felt sorry for me because of my earache, so he went to Harper's Appliances and bought me a record player. Can you believe it?"

The last time I was sick I got homemade popsicles that Mom made by filling the ice cube trays with Kool-Aid and sticking the cubes with toothpicks. And I had the mumps and was out for two weeks. So the answer was no, I couldn't believe her dad gave her a record player for having an earache.

Still, it's hard not to be excited about a new record player. And one that's Bernadette's very own. What would it be like to have a record player and no one hovering over you, telling you to not scratch the records?

"You could ask for some rock and roll records for your birthday."

"Oh, I don't want to wait that long. And it's not rock *and* roll, Marjorie. It's *rock 'n roll* now. You say it like it's all one word. I want to get Bill Haley and the Comets. Mom said maybe, but she won't let any of that Negro rock 'n roll in the house. She says it's too wild." Bernadette rolls her eyes. I shake my head.

Mothers. Only some mothers can be worse than others.

I don't understand what Mrs. Ferguson has against Negroes. I don't know any Negroes, personally. I've watched Amos and Andy and the Kingfish and the singer Harry Belafonte on television and they seem nice enough. But there are no Negroes at my school, at church, or in the grocery store by my house. Only when Mom, Carol Anne, and I put on our white gloves and take the bus downtown to shop at Hudson's do I see colored families, and they don't seem wild at all.

There's a line in Detroit and it's called Eight Mile Road. All the colored families live south of that line. You don't have to be Negro to live south of Eight Mile—lots of white folks live in Greektown and the Polish area called Hamtramck—but you have to be white to live north of it. About the only thing I know about Negroes is that I really like Negro music. Bernadette does, too, even if her mom won't let her bring it in the house.

The list of what and who Mrs. Ferguson lets in her house is long and complicated. Like she won't let Phyllis Brandt in the house, because Phyllis's mom is divorced and wears red Capri pants. And she won't let hamburger in the house, because who knows what all the grocery grinds up in there. Definitely no Italians or people who come up North from the South to work at the auto plants—doesn't matter whether they're white or colored. She calls them factory rats and they are definitely not allowed anywhere near *her* house. And no Lutherans, of course.

"My sister's friend Claudia? She has Fats Domino, Ray Charles, and everything. Maybe she'll let me borrow the records for a sleepover sometime," Bernadette whispers, like she's telling me a dangerous secret.

"That would be neato," I answer, trying out a new word I heard on the radio.

"If you bought some records with your Christmas money, I'd let you play them on my record player."

"I loaned all my money to Mr. Papadopoulos on Saturday night," I say.

"That's not smart, Marjorie. My parents didn't give him a single dime because even though those hillbillies in West Virginia pop out babies left and right, it's just plain wrong to sell them to any old person."

"Mr. and Mrs. Papadopoulos? They aren't just any old people." I can't believe she's saying this. Mom was so happy about them finally being parents. I haven't seen the baby yet. They picked him up when he was only three hours old and drove him back home. They named him Alexander. "My mom says as long as the baby winds up in a home where he's loved, then that's okay."

"Just because your mom went to college does not mean she knows everything. My mom's going to ask her prayer circle to beg forgiveness for them because who does and doesn't get babies is God's business and Mr. and Mrs. P. are going straight to H-E-double hockey sticks. And that baby of theirs is nothing but a bastard."

"Bernadette!" I can't believe she said what she said. Bad words are definitely not allowed in Mrs. Ferguson's house. But something tells me home is exactly where Bernadette heard that bad word about the Papadopouloses' new baby. I don't say anything else.

The outside stairs to our school are worn down into soft dents. As we scuff up the steps and into the school, Inga appears at my side, quiet as a shadow.

"You're new," Bernadette says, looking at Inga. "Is this the girl you have to sit with now?" she asks me. Inga blushes as red as the scarf Grandma Mona knitted for me. The scarf I'm not wearing. The scarf that I buried in the bottom of the mitten basket so it wasn't hanging on the hook, begging Mom to tell me to put it on.

"This is Inga," I say. But Bernadette doesn't seem to hear, either because of the layers over her ears or because she's too busy calling out to friends. I enter the double doors of the school walking a tightrope between Inga and Bernadette, trying not to edge too close to either one of them.

My mind churns like a washing machine with all the things I could say: *Hey, Bernadette, remember that spy in the black hat? Funny thing. I'm pretty sure it was just Inga's dad, not a commie at all. And this is Inga. Doesn't she have pretty hair? She doesn't speak English that well, but she likes Curious George and she knows the story in French. Yes, she speaks German, too. No, I don't know what her dad did in the war*—my mind is babbling like my mother's mouth did when she met Inga's mom.

As I watch Bernadette reaching out to all her friends, I realize there is no way I can communicate what I know about Inga to Bernadette. She wouldn't understand. When it comes to Inga, it's like Bernadette and I don't even speak the same language. I say nothing.

At that moment, I wish more than anything that Inga could be as popular as Bernadette. Then she would have plenty of friends and it wouldn't be so important whether I was her friend or not. But the truth is, I am Inga's only friend, and I wish I could bury that fact as easily as I did my red scarf.

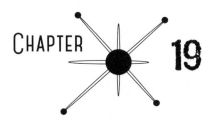

CHAPTER 19

"Bernadette, so glad you could join us today."

"I'm so happy to be back, Mrs. Kirk," Bernadette answers with a smile.

"Could you be so kind as to come to the board to write the answer to this morning's word problem?"

"Certainly." Bernadette pops up from her desk and fluffs her circle skirt before she starts up the aisle. She's wearing her circle skirt with the sombrero on it and at least three crinoline, stick-out petticoats. Kirk has a strict three petticoat rule and she's not shy about lifting up girls' skirts to count. She says any more than three is a hazard in our crowded classroom. I'm pretty sure that Bernadette is over the limit, since her skirt sticks out like an open umbrella, and when she swings her hips it swooshes from side to side. I feel the jolt when her hip hits Inga square in the shoulder as she passes by. I look up at Mrs. Kirk, but she has her back turned and is studying the board. Bernadette has perfect timing.

"So sorry," Bernadette says with a sniff and a little smile.

Only she's not sorry. She wants Inga to know who's boss.

Inga rubs her arm and looks at me with a question in her eyes. I fix my eyes on the board.

Bernadette writes, *The farmer has six sheep to sell at the market,* on the board. Mrs. Kirk's so excited that the answer's in a complete sentence that she claps three times and jumps up to underline the words on the blackboard. Her back's turned again when Bernadette swooshes back down the aisle to her seat. Inga's ready for her this time, and when Bernadette swings her hip, Inga leans in and gives her an elbow. Bernadette sprawls across Mike Tomaszeski's lap and all of his books dump on the floor. Bernadette whoops as she goes down with the clatter of books.

Mrs. Kirk spins. "What's this?" She sizes up the situation and asks, "Inga, did you just push Bernadette?"

Inga is silent.

"I tripped," says Bernadette. "Sorry, Mike." She rights herself and slides back to her desk without another single swish.

"That's very generous of you, Bernadette. Inga, you might as well know that I don't need eyes in the back of my head, I can read faces, and the color of your face tells me that you are up to no good. That kind of behavior will not be tolerated in my classroom, do you understand?"

"Yah," Inga says quietly.

"I beg your pardon? Did I just hear you apologize to Bernadette or didn't I?"

"Sorry," Inga says without hardly moving her lips or turning to look at Bernadette.

"I'll say you are sorry. There will be no more of that, little miss, is that understood?"

"Yah."

Everyone in the classroom except Mrs. Kirk knows that Bernadette hit Inga first. The room sits frozen, barely breathing.

I sit there with them, stiff and not touching Inga.

Mike bends to pick up his books and pencil. Mrs. Kirk turns back to the six sheep on the board.

From now on, it's official. This is war. Bernadette and Inga are enemies, only Inga doesn't know she can't win.

At recess, Mrs. Kirk makes Inga stay in to clean erasers with Owen Markey, who needs to be reminded that scissors are not toys.

Even I'm surprised at how quickly Bernadette starts to get kids on her side. She holds her arm and looks as if she's going to cry. I know Bernadette better than anyone and I'm sure that her arm is not hurt. I bet she was more than happy to have an excuse to sit on Mike Tomaszeski's lap, even if it was only for a second.

"I can't believe she did that to you," says Mary Virginia.

"Poor Bernadette," adds Piper, petting Bernadette like she's a cat.

"I can't believe you're friends with her," says Bernadette, looking at me with *how-could-you* hurt in her eyes.

I can't think of what to say, so I just shake my head. I'm waiting for Piper or Jodi or Mary Virginia or anyone to mention that Bernadette knocked Inga first. Hard. With her hip. I felt it. Is it possible that I'm the only one who knows this?

Everyone starts to talk about how Inga dresses. Her accent. Her hair. I say nothing. I am not shy, but sometimes I pretend I am. I pull my hood up and use the toe of my boot to kick a dent in the hardened snow. The bell rings.

For the past week, I have been explaining every assignment to Inga so that she can understand and keep up. Now with Bernadette's eyes burning into the back of my head, I am afraid to even look at Inga.

In the afternoon, Mrs. Kirk gives us four minutes of free time before the three o'clock bell. Bernadette comes over to our desk and announces in a loud voice that she's having a sleepover on Friday night. "You're coming, Marjorie, aren't you?" she asks.

My eyes slip to the side, looking at Inga.

"Oh, I see. You have to ask *her* permission before you say if you're going to sleep over at your best friend's house?"

"No," I say. Bernadette stands with her arms folded. "I'll be there."

"If you're not going to be happy about it, then don't bother," Bernadette says.

"I'm happy. I just . . ." I hesitate. "I'm just worried about . . . about . . . about stuff. Okay?"

"Let's not make this about you, Marjorie. You always want to turn things around. I have a new record player and stacks of records, and we're going to have loads of fun on Friday, right?" Bernadette pauses to look at Inga, who's quietly packing up her side of the desk. She looks back at me. "Everyone's going to be there. I'm so excited, aren't you?"

"Sure," I answer, trying to put a smile in my voice. Bernadette tells me that her mother's picking her up after school to go the doctor's, and then she turns on her heel, making her skirt stand out and flipping my spelling list off of the desk. By the time I pick it up and zip my pencils into their holder, Inga's at the coat rack. She leaves without saying good-bye. Part of me is relieved, and part of me wants to run after her.

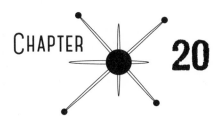

CHAPTER 20

If Bernadette can be sick for a week, then I can be sick for a week. Maybe by then things will have calmed down between Inga and Bernadette. I just need to look sick enough that Mom will keep me home. I had scarlet fever in second grade and was out for two weeks, just to make sure the shot worked and I didn't come down with rheumatic fever, which can ruin your heart.

I need a major illness, something that will keep me out of school for the rest of the year. Pauline Pothier was allowed to stay home for half a year in a body cast because she had curvature of the spine. I try standing crooked but don't look that convincing. I've already had mumps, chicken pox, and hard measles, so those excuses are out the window.

I go into the bathroom and swirl the hottest water I can stand in my mouth and stick the thermometer in before going downstairs. Dad hasn't left for work yet and is bent over the newspaper, sipping coffee. Mom's nowhere in sight, which is not good. She's easier to convince than Dad. Dad thinks if you want sympathy, you should look it up under *S* in the dictionary. But Dad doesn't even seem to notice me standing there.

"Lila, look here at this story in the paper," Dad says, pointing at a headline I can't read upside down. Mom comes to the dining room door, a piece of black toast in her hand, smelling like smoke.

"Looks like there was a theft over at the library last weekend."

Mom stands still. Frank pushes past her, holding a cup of coffee.

"Listen to this: '"This theft is a particularly heinous crime as these were books slated to be destroyed due to their anti-American content," says Head Librarian Mrs. Harvey Pearson.' Looks like more than a hundred books just disappeared. What do you think about that, Lila?" Dad looks up at Mom over his glasses.

"When was that?" asks Frank.

"They think it happened on Saturday," Dad answers. "No leads yet. But the cops don't always publish everything they know."

"Saturday afternoon?" asks Frank.

"That's what they're thinking, 'cording to this article. Is this what the pinko Friends of the Library were cooking up last week, Lila? You know anything about this?"

Frank, who usually talks to no one in the mornings, seems all excited about the story. "Books just disappeared? Books don't just walk off, somebody got to know what happened."

I take the thermometer out of my mouth before I bite down without thinking and break the glass. Mom holds her pose in the kitchen doorway.

"You 'spose that's a felony?" asks Frank. "I guess somebody might do some hard time over somethin' like that. Stealing's stealing."

"Says here there's going to be a thorough investigation," Dad says.

"Somebody's going to sing," says Frank. "Always happens

that way. One person sees their butt's on the line and they can't wait to snitch. Right Mrs. C.? Ain't that the way it always goes?"

"Don't say *ain't*, Frank." Nothing like bad grammar to kick-start Mom. She slips the burned toast into her apron pocket. "That's a big waste of time for the police, if you ask me. The books were just going to be thrown out anyway." A pause. "Anybody want more orange juice?"

"I guess that wasn't what I was asking you, Lila. I was asking if you know anything about this. Frank's right, stealing's stealing." Dad looks hard at Mom. "Like my mother always told me, right is right and wrong is nobody."

"Your mother also thinks that space aliens crashed in New Mexico, so I wouldn't necessarily—"

"Lila, just tell me you don't know anything."

"I know absolutely nothing." Mom turns back toward the kitchen. "And the longer I live, the less I know."

"Well, I don't guess Lydia Papadopoulos will be dragging you to any more subversive activities now that she's got that new baby, so I have nothing to worry about, right?"

Mom's already in the kitchen and turns on the water, a signal that from her perspective, the conversation's over. Frank's not done with it, though.

"Communist-leaning, them Greeks. Am I right?" Frank's on the edge of his chair, his leg bouncing up and down.

"I wouldn't say that." Dad answers.

"But they's kind of friendly with the Russians after the war, right?"

"Wasn't anybody friendly with the Russians after the war, boy. That's what the Cold War's all about."

"But the Greeks—"

"George and Lydia's good folks, Frank. All Greeks aren't commies, all Italians aren't Mafia thugs, and all Germans aren't Nazis. People are people; you got to take them one at a time. There's folks who'll tell you all Polacks are dumb, ain't got the sense God gave gravel. Your pop was one of the smartest men I've ever known, Polack through and through." Dad closes the newspaper and pushes his chair back. He wants the conversation to be over, too. Frank keeps talking.

"My pop said—" begins Frank.

"Your pop would'a said the same thing. No two people are the same. Even when it comes to soldiers, let me tell you. Not the same. Not the same at all. Your pop? He was good people, too." Dad sighs deep down. "Too good, maybe."

Dad stands, running his hand back and forth across the back of the chair. He sighs again. "The war was hard enough on him. Coming home, even harder. It's a damned sight easier to turn a shoe salesman into a killer than it is to turn a killer back into a human being." Dad stands and holds up two fingers. "I made myself two promises in the war, if I was lucky enough to return home. One, I was never going to camp out again in my life. No more rain in my mashed potatoes. Two, I'd never have a gun in the house. Never touch a gun again. I wish to God your dad had thought the same."

"My pop was a natural-born hunter, Nazis, deer, squirrel. All the same to him. He could knock the eye out of a Nazi or

136

a squirrel from two hundred yards." Frank sits like his spine is reaching toward the ceiling when he talks about his pop. He holds his head up proud.

"Your dad was always good with a rifle, from what he told me. But listen up, boy, killing people is nothing like shooting a deer or a squirrel, don't you ever believe it is. Deer don't shoot back, for one thing. In simple language, war's chaos, bullets flying, fire, noise. You can't think, you don't even want to think. Thinking can get you killed. After the smoke clears, that's when it all comes back on you."

My dad doesn't go to the VFW hall. VFW means Veterans of Foreign Wars and the so called "hall" is really a bar where vets go and hang out. Dad says that's just an excuse to drink too much and live in the past. He doesn't have much use for that. Except for kidding around now and then, I've never heard him talk about the war and what it was like. If someone else brings it up, it's never at breakfast. More like late at night when there's an open beer case in the kitchen. Dad always sends me to my room. This time, though, no one notices me standing there, thermometer dangling from one hand. I barely breathe.

"My pop was no chicken!" Frank's anger is never far from the surface, and right now it looks like it might bust out of him any minute.

"I'd never say that about your pop, or any other fighting man. I don't know what he saw or what he did, but I know this, your pop didn't do one bit more or less than any of the rest of us. Just another cog in the fighting machine, shooting at anything that moves because you want to stay alive another day. *It's the machine that kills,* you tell yourself, *I just work here.* And that machine killed Nazis, sure, but it also killed Frenchmen and Italians, shopkeepers, old folks with canes, and mothers and babies. No way in hell hunting deer prepares a man for that."

"But my pop made it home. He was a good soldier." Frank is close to crying. I can hear it in his voice. Dad is forever telling Frank what a good man his pop was. I can see Frank's eyes begging. He wants to hear it again.

"Yep, that he was. A good soldier. But surviving the shelling and the bullets, that's luck more than anything else. A fraction of an inch this way or that, and it's lights out." Dad snaps his fingers. "Quick as that. But the smells, the crying kids caught in the middle, the swollen bodies, that's what you can't shake—Marjorie, what in blazes are you doing standing there like a damned ghost?" Dad slams his open hand down on the dining room table. "Out! Upstairs and get dressed for school. Chop chop."

Before I can scramble back upstairs, Frank's out of his chair. Dad reaches to put a hand on Frank's shoulder, but Frank jerks away. He grabs his leather jacket off of the hook by the back door and slams out. We hear the kick start of his motorbike and then he roars down the drive.

I close my door before Dad has a chance to ask me if I know anything about the stolen books. Carol Anne, who is in afternoon kindergarten and has the mornings home alone with Mom, is sitting on her bed with her back toward me when I walk in the room. All her stuffed animals are lined up on her bed against the headboard.

"You better tell me who stole-ded all those books from the lib'ary," I hear her say in a bossy teacher voice, pointing her finger at the glassy-eyed animals. "Don't make me mad or you'll be sorry," she singsongs. She turns to look at me. "I know who took the books," she says.

"What?" I can't believe she's saying this. "Shh!"

"Mr. Toad took all the books and stacked them up like the Empire State Building."

My head feels like it will explode. I grab it with both hands. "Oh, grow up, Carol Anne."

CHAPTER 21

"Owen Markey, you will be partners with Marjorie. Inga, I want you to partner with Mr. Tomaszeski. Mary Virginia, you're with Sammy Bernstein." Mrs. Kirk checks us off in her book as she pairs us up boy/girl for a project in building relief maps of the Seven Wonders of the Ancient World. We don't have to build all seven, just put them on the map in the right place.

"I can work with Billy," Bernadette says, wagging her hand in the air.

"What? Oh, okay. I guess that's all right. Bernadette and Billy." Mrs. Kirk continues until everyone has a partner. She picks up a square tile off of a stack of them on her desk and holds it up for everyone to see. "If you happen to see Owen's father in the hallway or anywhere around town, I want you to thank him for generously donating these beautiful floor tiles for our project."

Owen stands and says, "My pop put his phone number on the back of each tile just in case anybody wants a new, modern kitchen floor."

"Thank you, Owen." Mrs. Kirk begins with the first row, passing out the tiles.

"Call Lincoln-6-3475, Markey Floors for a reliable and reasonable estimate, no charge."

"Thank you, Owen."

"Floors for any room in your house, not just the kitchen. My pop's been busy as a one-armed paper hanger flooring basement rec rooms."

"Sit, Owen."

"These are the biggest, most modern floor tiles ever made," Owen continues talking to me. He can't sit. He's too excited. "Eighteen inches square. See how smooth it is? Vinyl and asbestos, strong to last long."

"What should we do with it?" I ask him. We spread newspaper over my desk, place the tile in the middle, and just stare at it.

"I know, let's make a volcano," Owen says. "I saw it on *Mr. Wizard*. I know just how it works."

I look down at the list of the Seven Wonders of the Ancient World. Pyramid, Hanging Gardens, Statue of Zeus . . . no mention of a volcano. "I'm not sure that's what she wants," I say quietly.

"Sure it is. A volcano is what buried Pompeii. Kaboom!" Owen's arms fly up to the ceiling. "I can build the mountain out of asbestos tape. It doesn't burn. Neither will this tile. It won't even scratch."

"Burn?" I have never seen anyone set anything on fire at school before. In fact, I'm pretty sure lighting anything in class is against the rules.

"That's what real volcanoes do. They spit fire and rocks." Owen throws his palms up and looks at me like I'm an idiot.

"I know that, it's just we need to put the Mediterranean Sea, Egypt, and Greece in here, and—"

"Okay, you do that part. I'll build the mountain at home tonight and we can put it together tomorrow. This will be too

141

cool. Just like on *Mr. Wizard*. Here!" Owen says as he shoves the tile in my hands.

"But what about the Wonders?" I ask, only Owen doesn't hear me because he sits down to draw a jagged triangle with fire spitting out of the top. "Owen? The Wonders?" I tap his shoulder lightly.

"You can put those on there if you want. Make little flags or something."

"Do you two have a plan?" Mrs. Kirk asks as she drifts by, looking over her glasses at how different teams are busy sketching out where the hills will go on their relief maps that up to a couple of minutes ago were just floor tiles.

"We have the greatest plan ever, Mrs. Kirk. It's going to be a big surprise," Owen says.

"I just bet it will be," says Mrs. Kirk. She stops. Suddenly the air is electrified.

The wail begins low and races to a deafening high pitch, straining our ears and setting the entire class in motion. *WAAAAAAIIIIILLLLLL!*

"Red alert!" screams Owen.

"Red alert!" The words pass between us as the siren sounds. Piercing. Continuous. We all grab for our spelling books and line up against the wall. We file out into the hallway as all the other classrooms empty out. We take our practiced places, backs against the wall, heads between our knees, and spelling books over our heads.

"Cover your head, Mary. Jimmy, head between your knees. Owen, this is not a joke." Mrs. Kirk stands with a magazine open on top of her head, grade book in hand, making sure that all her ducks are in a row.

The siren's made right where Dad works, at Chrysler. He's told me all about it. It's a Chrysler Air Raid Siren. It weighs more than a car and is powered by a V8 engine. When it's fired up, it's so loud it can turn fog into rain and make birds fall right out of the sky on their heads. So loud you can hear it for twenty miles. Only we are just a few blocks from city hall, so it really blasts out our eardrums when it goes off. The wailing feels like ice picks in my head and lasts for three whole minutes. My ears are numb when it finally begins to drop to a low moan. I can barely hear the teacher.

"Where's Inga?" says Mrs. Kirk, looking back and forth, up and down the aisle. One of her ducks in a row is missing. "Inga?"

Principal Hawkins strides down the hall with a stopwatch in his hand. "Good work, children, excellent time. Everybody out in the hall, away from the windows in less than a minute and a half. Good job. Good job," he says, tapping students' heads as he walks along. He stops beside Mrs. Kirk, who's still wearing her *Life* magazine as a hat. "What's the matter?"

"I'm missing one."

"Oh, no! I'll have to include this in my report, Gertrude. What happened?"

"I don't know, that new girl, Inga." Mrs. Kirk rushes to the closed classroom door.

"Children. Everybody stand. Back inside." Mr. Hawkins opens his arms wide as if he's trying to lasso the entire class. "Come. Come."

The door swings open and we all crowd in and stand in a cloud by the door. "Inga?" calls Mrs. Kirk. "Shh," she orders the rest of us. "Silence. Inga?"

"Over there," Mike says. He points to the far corner of the room where a cabinet door is open a crack. The cloud of kids starts to move, but Mr. Hawkins tells us to stay back. He and Mrs. Kirk bend down to look in the cabinet. He opens the door wide. Straining, I can see Inga, all balled up. Mrs. Kirk kneels down. "Oh, Inga. Inga. It's just a test. Come on, honey." Inga lifts her head for a second and sees us all staring and buries her head back in her knees, her shoulders sobbing. "Come along, child," Mr. Hawkins says. He reaches for her, but doesn't touch her. It's Mrs. Kirk who gently tugs on Inga, coaching her out. She sits down flat on the floor and pulls Inga into her arms. We're all quiet. Even Owen Markey for once has nothing to say. Mrs. Kirk rocks balled-up Inga, holding her in a hug as the whole class watches for an uncomfortable couple of minutes.

"Okay, you all know where you are supposed to be," says Mr. Hawkins. "I suggest you go there."

No one says a word, but no one moves either. My eyes catch Bernadette's, and I can see a smile starting to gather around her mouth. She's trading elbow jabs with Mary Virginia, and both of them are bending over trying to catch what's happening with Inga.

"Did she fall or something?" I hear Owen ask Mike.

"No, man. She just dove into that cabinet headfirst. She was like a streak of lightning. Soon as the siren hit," answers Mike. "She okay?" he asks Mrs. Kirk.

"Maybe she just tripped over her stockings," Mary Virginia

says in a whisper designed to be loud enough for everyone to hear.

"Guess there's no such thing as air raid drills in Can-a-da," Bernadette says in a singsong voice.

"Hush up, you girls. Go on back to your seats. I don't want to have to tell you another time," Mr. Hawkins says in his principal voice.

Mrs. Kirk whispers in Inga's ear, "It's okay, sweetheart. You're just fine. It's just a test. Shh, shh." Inga sobs into Mrs. Kirk's shoulder and the biggest part of me wants to put my arms around her, but the smaller part of me that lives in my shoes doesn't move.

Mrs. Kirk doesn't seem to be bothered about showing us her bare knees. She ties her stockings under her knees rather than holding them up with garters like the rest of the world, a fact we all discovered thanks to swirling winds on the playground in September. Everybody talked about it for a week. Knees are a part of a teacher kids are not supposed to see, so I can't help staring at her sprawled on the floor, arms and legs out like an octopus with white knees.

"Move it!" Hawkins orders. I bolt to my desk.

I finally see Inga nod, and they both stand up, Mrs. Kirk smoothing her dress back down where it belongs. Her arm is still wrapped around Inga's shoulders.

"Inga would like to come down to the office and have a little glass of water with you, Mr. Hawkins," she says, looking into Inga's face. Inga nods.

"Yes. Well. Of course." Mr. Hawkins nods briskly and again reaches toward Inga. They walk out of the door with his arm almost around her shoulders, but not quite touching. She's still holding one hand over her mouth and she's breathing in little gasps and sniffling.

It's true that this new air raid siren blasts so loud it makes the fillings in my teeth hurt. It was installed right after Christmas. We are all used to these tests. I suppose it scared Inga since she's new, but I have no idea why she didn't follow the rest of us into the hallway and away from the windows and the fallout in case it really had been an H-bomb.

As scary as that air raid siren might be if you have never heard one before, I can't imagine why it would have made Inga jump into that cabinet and curl up in a ball. And everyone was looking at her. All I can think is that she must be so embarrassed. I'm embarrassed for her.

"You are allowed to take your project home overnight, but you have to bring it back tomorrow," Mrs. Kirk reminds everyone at the end of the day. "You may use papier–mâché or real rocks for your mountains, but no real water in the Mediterranean, okay? That's the rule. Too messy. What did I say?"

"No real water in the Mediterranean," we respond in unison. Kirk makes us repeat stuff back when she wants us to remember something really important. I want to ask her if real fire is okay, but she passes by too quickly and I don't want to shout it out. Everyone would look at me.

I pick up Carol Anne after school and go by the office to see if Inga's still there, but she's gone. I want to ask the secretary if Inga's mom came to pick her up early, but the office is jammed with people and there's a line to use the phone. I grab the hood of Carol Anne's coat and steer her toward the door. If Inga had a phone at her house, I think maybe I could stand in line to call her.

Bernadette's heading to Mary Virginia's house after school, and I watch them walk down the school steps, shrieking with laughter. I don't exactly know what they think is so funny, but I can guess. Inga.

Since it's just me and Carol Anne walking home, I consider stopping by Inga's house to see if she's okay. I make Carol Anne stand with me on Inga's corner for a few minutes while I think it over.

"Fly below the radar, Margie girl, but never try and fly below ground level." My father loves to give me canned advice. Like when he tells me, "Lead, follow, or get out of the way." That's one of his favorites.

I've never been quite sure what he meant by "fly below the radar but not below ground level," but standing here, I think if anyone, *anyone*, were to see me walking to Inga's house, that would definitely not be flying under the radar. It might even be trying to fly below ground level. My reputation would crash and burn. I'd be cracked up. Done for.

Guilt over Inga. Air raid sirens. Owen and his idiotic volcano. Carol Anne yanking on my arm. I'm feel as if I'm stretched in fifteen different directions.

"Stop pulling on me!" The words burst out of me like a thunderclap.

"I'm cold, Marjorie. Let's gooooo," Carol Anne whines.

"Gimme a minute, I'm trying to think."

"Think at home." She pulls at my arm, leaning with all of her weight. I pull back until I feel my feet start following after her. I tell myself there's no time to go to Inga's house because I have too much homework now that I'm stuck having to draw the map of the ancient world all by myself. But I know that's only part of it.

If I start talking to Inga again, it would be too hard to explain to Bernadette.

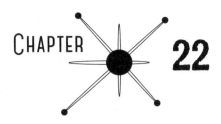

CHAPTER 22

"Did they rebuild Pompeii in the same place after the volcano?" I ask Mom. I am sitting at the kitchen table, copying the coastline from one of my maps onto the tile. It's after dinner and Mom's doing dishes. She comes to look over my shoulder, her pink rubber gloves dripping on the floor.

"I have no idea, pumpkin," she says. "Go ask your father. He's been to Greece." She picks up a pot off of the stove and plunges it into the dishwater.

"Pompeii's in Italy, Mom."

"Your dad's been there, too."

I pick up my map and trudge down the hall to the living room, where Dad is dozing in his chair. No one else is in the room since Dad's the only one who likes to watch *See It Now* with Edward R. Murrow. Dad would watch the news all day and night if he didn't have to work, except maybe if the Red Wings were playing. I stand in the doorway and look at the black-and-white image on the screen. It looks like the same report as every other night. A senator named McCarthy is speaking into a microphone. Everyone knows who Senator McCarthy is. He's on TV and on the front page of the newspaper every day. Mostly he's famous for asking people if they are now or ever were a member of the Communist Party. Whatever he's talking about this time, he has the whole place laughing like it's *I Love Lucy*, which makes no sense to me.

McCarthy says, "A few days ago, I read that President Eisenhower expressed the hope that by election time in 1954 the subject of communism would be a dead and forgotten issue. The raw, harsh, unpleasant fact is that communism is an issue and will be an issue in 1954."

I look over at Dad. Usually the word *communism* makes him sit up straight in his chair and lean toward the TV set, but he's sound asleep. I stand in the doorway as the news broadcast switches back and forth from McCarthy to Edward R. Murrow. Each time McCarthy is questioning a different person.

"Nothing is more serious than a traitor to this country in the communist conspiracy," says McCarthy, and the whole place explodes in applause.

I gulp.

Does keeping a box of books under my bed make me a traitor? I wonder. If *1984* and *The Grapes of Wrath* and all the other books are pro-communist, does hiding them make me part of the communist conspiracy? Could Mom and I and Mrs. Papadopoulos be called before the whole Senate? Who would take care of her new baby? If Mom went to jail, Carol Anne would explode like a feather pillow. I start to chew on my thumbnail.

McCarthy is talking to an Army guy now. "And wait till you hear the bleeding hearts scream and cry about our methods of trying to drag the truth from those who know, or should know, who covered up a Fifth Amendment Communist, Major. But they say, 'Oh, it's all right to uncover them, but don't get rough doing it, McCarthy.'"

Methods? What methods? How will they try to drag the truth out of me? Is making fun of a person on TV what he means by the words *get rough*, or would there be a windowless room with a table and a bare light bulb like in the movies? He wants to drag Fifth Amendment Communists out of dark recesses and expose them to the public. If he dragged me out of the dark, I'd have no defense. Kids are never allowed to plead the Fifth Amendment about anything. If I said I didn't want to incriminate myself, I'd be grounded until I spilled my guts.

"And upon what meat doth Senator McCarthy feed?" Murrow asks.

I picture the Senator chewing on my leg like a chicken bone.

Some other guy who wrote a book in 1932 says, "I think Communists are, in effect, a plainclothes auxiliary of the Red Army, the Soviet Red Army. And I don't want to see them in any of our schools, teaching." It sounds like the right thing to say, but anybody can see he's still in trouble.

I had never thought about communists teaching in the United States. Were there communist teachers at Homer Elementary? Mrs. Kirk wouldn't fit into a Red Army uniform, I don't think. I imagine her sausage-squeezed into a jacket with the buttons popping off instead of in one of her flowered dresses, but shake the image out of my head. Communist teachers don't seem real to me. But communist books I have heard about. I have a box of them under my bed.

Slam. The basement door. Before I can even picture Frank entering the kitchen, Dad jerks in his chair, and flies up, on his feet.

He's across the room. His arms swing out as he twirls like a windmill.

Crash. The floor lamp smashes on the floor and goes out.

In the darkness, Dad screams, "DOWN! DOWN! GET DOWN!"

Dad's screaming sets an air raid siren off in my head. I crumple to my knees and cover my head with my arms. *Down. Down.* The room is blackness. I can feel the vibrations from Dad's feet through the floor. Too scared to move, I clutch at my ears and roll into a tight ball.

"Get . . . get . . . what? Oh, good lord." Dad's voice sounds cloudy and confused. "Damnation," he shouts and pounds his fist into the wall. "Damn. Damn. Damn." Pound. Pound. Pound. A picture crashes to the floor.

More shattering glass. I shrink smaller, tighter.

"Jack?" Mom's voice. Her feet rush past me. I peek through my hair.

Dad leans, one hand against the wall, and one still clutching his forehead. "Good God," he's panting like he just ran up the stairs six times. "Ugh." Mom's at his side, arm around his waist. I hear her whispering.

"Everything okay?" It's Frank.

Mom's told me that sometimes bombs go off in Dad's head. It's like the war starts booming around him and he has to yell and kick to make it go away. The dreams come in the middle of the night or in the living room in his chair if he's surprised and wakes up too fast.

I hear another lamp switch on. A yellow glow seeps through the dark living room and between my arms, which are still wrapped around my head.

"Little problem here," says Frank. He must be pointing at me, but I can't really see much. I'm buried in the cave of my arms. The whine of engines overhead, the tat-tat-tat of anti-aircraft fire, explosions all around me. Every war newsreel and movie I have ever seen are playing in my mind at the same time.

"Oh, baby," Mom says, kneeling beside me. "Oh, don't cry. It's all over. Don't cry."

Only I do. I cry. I don't cry like a baby, either. I cry like the Chrysler Air Raid Siren. I cry like I'm going to explode into an H-bomb mushroom cloud. I cry in gasping sobs, like I am trapped in a cabinet and can't catch my breath. I cry like I was just arrested for being a commie traitor. I cry like police have come to drag my mother to jail in her bathrobe. I cry like Mom when she had her bad spell and lived in the bedroom for three weeks and Grandma Mona had to come and take care of us. I cry, palms tight against my eyes.

Dad scoops me up and puts me in a ball on the sofa, while I keep crying. He tells me, "It's okay. It's okay," smoothing his hand over my back. "Come on, baby. Daddy didn't mean to scare you. It's okay." He rocks me back and forth a few times, and then he says, "I can't take this right now, Lila."

"Let me," Mom says, sitting beside me.

Dad pulls out his handkerchief and wipes his face. I hear him

153

blow his nose as he leaves to go out in the garage. If I didn't know better, I would think that he's crying, too. But Dad has always told me that good soldiers don't cry, even soldiers who aren't soldiers anymore. Frank follows after him.

Carol Anne's been hiding under the dining room table, but now she slides up on the sofa with Mom and me and nuzzles into our hug.

"Breathe," Mom says. The air seems to have knots in it, but I try to choke it in.

Each time she tells me that it's okay, more tears burn down my face.

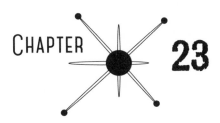
Mom holds out a small square envelope to me as I'm on the way out the door to school the next morning. On it she's written *Mrs. Scholtz* in her perfect handwriting with her favorite green fountain pen. I stare at it.

"The bridge club is having a little shower for the Papadopouloses' new baby. I thought your new friend's mother might like to join us. Just give Mrs. Scholtz's invitation to Inga."

"I have too much to carry," I say, holding out my tile map. The project looks pretty pathetic in the morning light. Mom made me cocoa after the thing with Dad last night. A milkshake would have been better, but with no ice cream in the house, she said hot chocolate would just have to do. Then she helped me finish the map before bed. We glued mounds of tissues for the relief mountains and poked colored toothpicks into them to mark the locations of the Seven Wonders. I made a legend on a separate piece of paper explaining what was what. The map only shows the heel of the boot that is Italy, so I don't exactly know where the volcano is going to go and hope, hope, hope that Owen forgets to bring it.

"Take this envelope, Marjorie. Don't be silly. Here," and she shoves the invitation in my coat pocket.

Bernadette is carrying her project, too, when we meet up at the end of my driveway. We look like waitresses holding our trays. Hers has papier-mâché mountains and blue aluminum foil covering the Mediterranean Sea. She has built a perfect pyramid out of cardboard and put blocks on the sites of the other Wonders. I wish I had thought of blocks because my toothpicks are looking pretty shaky in the morning breeze.

Bernadette whines that hers hasn't had enough time to dry. "Billy and I had to paint the mountains when they were still wet. He came over to my house last night, and we worked on it together. Can you believe that Kirk didn't give us two nights for this project? It's not fair." She looks at my tile with the wobbly toothpicks and says nothing.

It's not like I think I'm going to marry Billy or anything. Grandma Mona told me that Catholic boys never marry Presbyterians. She says Catholics are all liars and all they want is to kiss you and then they drop you like a hot potato. She says Catholics can't be trusted because they only do what the Pope tells them to do, and wherever you find four Catholics, you always find a fifth, because all Catholics are drunks. She told me that I should marry a nice Jewish boy because they are good family men. Or I should marry a sober Methodist. That was right about when Mom decided her bad spell was over and Grandma Mona should go back to Ohio.

A bad spell isn't getting the word *Massachusetts* wrong on a test. A bad spell is when a person starts crying and doesn't want to open the curtains. After Grandma Mona left, Mom told us not to worry, she wasn't ever going to cry again, which we all knew wasn't true, but we went along with it to try and make her be happy again.

Bernadette and I walk, holding our tile projects. I try not to be upset because Billy O'Brien came over to Bernadette's house. I don't know what it is about Billy. He just makes my insides skip around, and for a second I let myself think about what it would have been like to build my project with him in *my* kitchen. Before I can imagine us laughing and stirring up papier-mâché, I think about Mom and how she laughed until she cried last night when she found the piece of burned toast in her apron pocket. I think about Dad and the broken lamp. Carol Anne, who practically lives under the dining room table—and Frank.

Right then I know Billy O'Brien will always be the boy who delivers our paper but who never comes inside the house, which is probably a good thing. Still, it might have been fun. Instead I had to be paired with Owen Markey.

By the time we arrive at school I have managed to lose three toothpicks. Fortunately, I packed spares in my pocket. I hang my coat on the hook in the back of the classroom and put the tile on my desk.

When I return to my coat and dig around in the pocket for the spare toothpicks, the invitation comes out, too. The square white envelope drops silently to the floor. I look around to see if anyone notices, but luckily everyone is busy setting up their projects along the window ledge. I walk away from the envelope.

So far, no sign of Owen. The first bell rings. The first bell means everyone should be in school except the safety patrol, and they have three minutes to hightail it in before the second bell. Since Owen was kicked off the safety patrol last fall for chasing leaves instead of helping kindergarteners cross the road, he's supposed to be here.

I sigh with relief, hoping he's come down with something really sickening overnight, like the plague of Egypt. Some disease with spots and a fever and swollen glands that would keep him and his Mr. Wizard volcano home for the rest of the week. I wish the Seven Wonders of the Ancient World never existed. I want to forget this project and go back to diagramming sentences, which I can do all on my own, with no one watching me.

I put the tile on my desk and use the legend to replace the toothpicks to match the Wonders, attempting to fix what the wind had messed up on the walk to school before adding it to the other projects on the window ledge.

"Where's your partner, Margie?" asks Bernadette. Before I can say, "I hope he's in the hospital," the door opens and in walks Owen, carrying his mountain on its own tile.

"No fair," Bernadette squawks. "Owen and Marjorie used two tiles."

Billy, Mike, Sammy, and the other boys don't seem to care about the second tile. Instead they crowd around Owen saying things like, "Cool" and, "Neat," and Sammy even whistles. Owen comes over and carefully slides the mountain smack in the middle of the Mediterranean I have carefully drawn on our official tile. He drops the spare tile on the ground.

"Hey," I say. But Owen doesn't hear me. He's talking to the growing crowd of boys gathering around my desk and the mountain.

"Wait. Wait," he says. "Wait till you see the best part."

"Is this the volcano from the Mr. Wizard show?" asks Sammy.

"Soda and vinegar, big deal," says Billy.

"Wrong-o," Owen says. "This is a fire volcano. I stuffed it with ammonium dichromate from my chemistry set and added smashed-up sparklers."

"Cool," the boys say in unison.

Right then is when I know I should shout for the teacher. Right at that moment, I know I should scream. But part of me is too scared to speak and a little part of me wants to see what ammoni-whatever-it-is does to sparklers.

Owen shrugs his coat off and flings it to the side before reaching into his pocket. "This is so cool, you won't believe it. Too bad it's not dark in here." In one hand I glimpse a silver Zippo lighter, in the other he holds the end of a string fuse that leads to a hole in his mountain. "Stand back," he orders. "Silence."

Mrs. Kirk, who's bent over the trash can looking for something, stands straight up when she hears the silence. The unmistakable click of a lighter brings her running.

"What's going on here," she says as she rushes over, making her way through the jungle of kids, swinging her arm like a blunt machete. "Did I hear a lighter?"

The lighter has disappeared.

A small flame zips along, gobbling up the fuse.

"You can't," she screams. But it's too late.

The mountain erupts, spitting sparks straight up in a plume of smoke. Owen's face opens in a wide smile. The stream of fire continues to burst from his asbestos mountain, casting a warm light on his proud face.

"Holy Mary, Mother of God," Mrs. Kirk shrieks. "Everybody out!"

We jump back, but no one heads towards the door. Everyone's eyes are fixed on the flying sparks. By the time Mrs. Kirk throws Owen's coat over the mountain, it's already started to fizzle out.

The class erupts with applause. I'm not sure if they're clapping for the volcano or Kirk's heroic coat move.

"Whose desk is this?" she demands. She's all red in the face and the last thing in the world I want to say is whose desk it is.

"It's Marjorie's," Bernadette says.

"Marjorie Campbell, principal's office. Owen Markey? Was this your idea?"

"It's asbestos, Mrs. Kirk. It's okay, it won't burn." Owen scrubs the air with his hands, trying to calm her down.

"Oh, yeah? See your classmates? See their clothes. Guess what?" She grabs Owen by the shirt collar and hisses into his ear. "They burn, Mr. Markey. Kids burn, do you understand?" At that moment, I'm glad Mrs. Kirk doesn't have control of the Zippo lighter. I'm afraid she might demonstrate just how easily kids burn, specifically Owen. "The lighter. In my hand. Now."

Owen slowly reaches into his pocket. "It's my dad's. You can't keep it, he'll kill me if it gets lost."

Mrs. Kirk snatches the lighter away from him before he has a chance to put it in her hand. "Mr. Hawkins gets to kill you first. Principal's office."

"But I didn't do it," I complain.

"Did you know about this?" Mrs. Kirk asks, her eyes burning into me.

"Not exactly," I say. "I mean—"

"You mean *nothing*. Why didn't you say something? Don't you know better than to stand by while someone does something dangerous and not say anything? He could have set the whole school on fire! What's the matter with you, Marjorie?

"And you!" She still has Owen by the collar.

We are heading for the classroom door when Mrs. Kirk's lace-up high heel slips on a small white envelope. "Yipe!" she barks, and almost goes down flat. "What's this?" She steadies herself and bends to pick the envelope up, reading it in a glance. "Scholtz!" she bellows. "Inga, take this out of my hand. Now."

Inga rushes over.

"I swear you kids are trying to kill me. Here." She jabs the envelope into Inga's hand.

Mrs. Kirk shoves Owen and me into the hallway. "Wait here for one minute and do not move." To the rest of the class, "I will be back in a couple of minutes. Do not touch *anything* and do not set the room on fire. What did I say?" she screams.

"Don't set the room on fire," the class yells back.

I follow Kirk's clomping shoes down the marble hallway to the principal's office. This is my first trip to the office because I am actually in trouble. I'm not sure what happens in the principal's office. Whatever it is happens to Owen on a pretty regular basis. He always comes back, so I figure Mr. Hawkins isn't going to actually kill me. Still, I wish I could melt away and not be noticed, but that isn't going to happen, either.

The words I hear rumbling like faraway thunder in my head are Mrs. Kirk saying, "You mean nothing." As I walk along, shoulders slumped, I think her words just about sum up my whole life. A big zero.

At least the invitation was delivered. But I couldn't even do that.

Mrs. Kirk's right. I am nothing. A nobody. Big fat zero. A circle with air inside.

I hold her words in my clasped hands as we sit in the principal's office. At the end of the day, I tuck the words into my hat with my ponytail and carry them home with me. These are the words that I hang on the hook by the back door with my coat when I get home.

I mean nothing.

I trudge up to my room wearing the words like a heavy sign around my neck.

"Marjorie," Mom calls up the stairs. "Be a doll and run down to the basement and give those pillowcases a stir, will you? And don't let that bleach water splash on your skirt."

"No," I scream back. "Make Carol Anne do it."

"Thanks, sweetheart."

She just assumes I'll just go along with what she asks. Everyone assumes I'll just go along. That's what nothings do.

They just go along. I feel my hands going into fists as I start down the two flights of stairs.

I clomp down to the first floor and then down the wooden basement stairs and into the laundry room. In the white metal bucket that used to be Carol Anne's diaper pail stands a wooden broomstick that I use to swirl the soaking pillowcases.

I am mad enough to kick the bucket across the floor, but I stir the milky looking mixture of soap, bleach, and pillowcases slowly and stand the broomstick in the corner before heading for the stairs. Coming out of the laundry room, I can't avoid looking into the area that's been converted into Frank's bedroom. He has a gym bag on his bed. He's stuffing in a pair of jeans.

"Are you running away from home or something?" I try not to sound too excited.

"Don't be sticking your nose in where it don't belong, Squirt."

"*Doesn't.* I guess Dad might want to know if you're going somewhere," I say, reaching for the handrail to pull myself up the basement stairs.

"I'm going to take the bike over to Jackson to visit my brother, like it's any of your business. And you're not going to tell your dad about my plans. You got that? Better to ask for forgiveness than permission. I'm just going to go up there and check on Charles, make sure his head's straight and be right back."

"And I'm not going to tell Dad that you're taking a motorcycle to Jackson? Ha. That's what you think." I jump the first stair on my way up.

"I guess your pop might want to know that you and your

mom hid a box of those missing books in your bedroom, too, now wouldn't he? Or maybe I should just go straight to the police."

I am a statue.

He pulls a green book out of his gym bag and shoves it toward my face. "Look familiar?"

I am a statue with a heart pounding like ten thousand drums.

"This Hemingway guy's hep. Doesn't talk over your head, ya know what I mean?" He jams the book back in his bag. "Didn't think I could read, did ya."

I blink.

"Yeah. I know a lot more than you think I know, so don't go acting all smarter than thou on me."

"You've been in my room?" I lean forward as I throw the words at him in a hoarse whisper. I wish I had something else to throw. *He was under my bed?*

"You were under my bed?"

"Hey, it don't take a college professor to put two and two together. I was standing next to the dining room window, having a sandwich, when you and your mom pull in the drive and proceeds to carry a heavy box up to your room. I think, how come they don't ask for help with that box? How come, if grocery bags weigh more than a roll of toilet paper, I'm called to carry them in from the car? And here she comes, leaning back so as to fall over, carrying a box looks like it weighs a ton and a half? Big mystery, right?

"And then I hear that a box of books has gone missing

from the library. And don't you know, both a these things, they happen on the same day. So, yeah. I thought I'd take a look's all. Maybe read one, just for kicks. This here's the third book I took. This Hemingway, he's a guy's guy. Damned sight better than the stinking Jane Austen they keep trying to cram down my throat at school." He looks at me, a wicked smile pulling his mouth to one side. "Don't let a bird fly in that open mouth a yours. He might crap all over."

I pinch my mouth together so nothing incriminating slips out. Frank's been under my bed. Three times! He knows about the books?

Three times?

"Got nothing to say now, do ya? Didn't think so. Now go upstairs and be a good girl or I'll blow your secret to kingdom come."

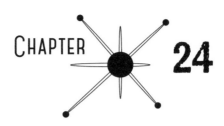

CHAPTER 24

"It wasn't that bad," I answer honestly. At Bernadette's sleepover, all the girls want to hear what happened when I was sent to the principal's office. Like being president of the student council or on the safety patrol, the principal's office is a spot reserved for boys. I am the first girl I ever heard of to be sent there.

How can I tell them about how Mr. Hawkins sat down right beside Owen and asked him what happened? How Hawkins wanted to know about the ammonium stuff and how Owen got his hands on it. How Hawkins asked what else Owen liked to cook up with his chemistry set and if he ever tried mixing this chemical with that one to make crystals. Hawkins made a pretty big deal out of telling Owen that he didn't ever want him to bring a lighter to school again, and that was really the worst of it. Owen promised, scout's honor, no more lighters.

Then Owen asked for the lighter back. I couldn't believe he had the nerve to even ask, but looking at his face, he looked like he might cry. He didn't cry, because he's Owen, but he looked like he might. He said it was engraved and that it had gone to the Philippines and back with his dad. "It's his lucky lighter," Owen pleaded. Hawkins turned the lighter over in his hand to look at the engraving.

"Well, out of respect to your dad and all the boys who went

overseas, I'm going to give this back to you. You just come by and see me after school and then you go straight home with it and don't be setting anything else on fire."

Owen promised again, scout's honor.

Then Hawkins told us we should sit in the lobby for fifteen more minutes before returning to class. Finally he told Owen to try to go a little easier on Mrs. Kirk because he was *this close* to stretching her nervous system to the breaking point. Owen agreed. Owen said he didn't want to break Mrs. Kirk. Really.

It wasn't until Hawkins stood up because it was time for us to leave that he finally he looked at me and asked, "And what's your name, little lady?"

"Marjorie Campbell," I whispered.

"Okay, Miss Campbell. I don't ever want to see you in my office again unless it's to use the pay phone, is that understood?" I nodded, and that was that.

Now, it's Friday night, school's locked up tight for the weekend, and there are four girls looking straight at me. We are in the Fergusons' basement rec room, taking a break from dancing to Bernadette's new record player. Mary Virginia, Piper, Jodi Solomon, and even Bernadette want to hear what it's really like in the principal's office.

"It's like a dungeon," I say.

"Really?" says Mary Virginia. All the girls bend into my words, waiting to hear about the horrors of Hawkins's dungeon.

"He pulls the curtains first, so no one can see in. It's almost totally dark."

Everyone gasps. "Did he torture you and Owen at the same

time?" Piper asks. She's chewing her lip like bubble gum.

Everyone knows Mr. Hawkins has a paddle hanging prominently on his wall. You can see it from the hallway when his door's open. The paddle has holes in it so he can smack harder with less wind resistance.

"Did you get the paddle?" Jodi asks. "Girls first?"

"You aren't allowed to paddle girls," Bernadette says. "Not even if you're a principal."

Bernadette always talks like she knows so much. Only this time I know more about something than she does, even though she has two older sisters, two cars, and a record player. I know because I have been there, and everybody else knows it, too.

"Weeellll," I begin slowly. "First he made both of us—"

"Kneel on the ground," says Piper. "That's what he does, right?" Piper is nervously chewing on her thumb cuticle.

"Right," I say.

"I knew it," Piper says. "He puts gravel on the floor and makes you kneel on it."

"And then did he take the paddle down off the wall?" asks Jodi.

I nod.

"I would have been so scared, I would have peed my pants," says Mary Virginia.

"I almost did," I say.

"But he didn't hit you," Bernadette says.

"He didn't have to," Mary Virginia says. "You don't have to smack people if you already have them scared to death."

168

"Exactly," Jodi says, slapping her thighs.

"That's his whole plan, don't you see? To keep everyone scared. Then he doesn't really have to swat us because we're too scared to do anything wrong," Bernadette says. "He has so many kids in that school, what's he supposed to do? He's one against hundreds." She shrugs. Obviously she's not scared of Mr. Hawkins.

"Well, I think it's a pretty good plan," Jodi says. "Did he hit Owen at least?"

Before I can answer, Bernadette plops a square spiral notebook down in the middle of our little conversation circle on the floor. "Guess what this is?"

The obvious answer is that it's a spiral notebook, but none of us bothers to say that. Clearly, it must be something else.

Bernadette looks at each of us before saying, "It's called a slam book."

"A what?" We all answer together.

"A slam book. It's something they have in junior high and my sister told me all about them. You have to know about them." Bernadette lays her hand on the book like she's swearing on a Bible to tell the truth, the whole truth, and nothing but the truth.

"What's in it?" I ask.

"Nothing," says Bernadette. "Nothing yet, that is."

"Oh, I get it. We use this book to slam boys in the head just to get their attention," says Mary Virginia. Mary Virginia is quick—with seven brothers and sisters, she has to be. If you asked our class to point out the most sarcastic person in the room, everyone would point to Mary Virginia.

169

"Okay," Bernadette sighs, "It goes like this. We decide a person we want to write about and put her name in the front of the book. Then we take turns asking questions about that person and also take turns writing answers to the questions. We pass it around. The only rule is that the questions and answers all have to be about the person whose name is in the front of the book. Oh, and one question per page, so you leave plenty of room for answers."

"That's two rules," says Mary Virginia.

Bernadette gives her a playful push and says, "Be serious, this is going to be so much fun. Only we have to keep it secret."

That's three rules, I think, but I don't say it out loud. "Is the person who the book is about allowed to answer the questions?" What if someone made a slam book about me and asked how I wound up with a big brother with a motorcycle? I'd want to be the one to answer the question before someone else had a chance to make something up.

My brain skips to wondering how Frank is doing, riding in the cold. I wonder if his face has frozen off or if his hands are numb. I see the taillight of his motorcycle disappearing into the darkness and shrinking smaller and smaller until it's only a blood red pinprick in the night. If I didn't hate Frank so much, I might even be a little worried about him, but I shrug that off. Like he said, he's old enough to look out for himself.

"You don't get it," Bernadette says. "She doesn't see the book until it's all done, and then we can give it to her or not. We decide that later. Here, look." Bernadette opens the spiral. *Inga Scholtz* is written on the first page in purple crayon. Bernadette flips the first page over to where she's already written the first question.

Why does Inga wear her braids wrapped around her head like a crown?

"I know," Jodi says. "She thinks she's queen of the universe."

"No," Mary Virginia says, shifting up onto her knees. "She does that to cover her horns. She's a red devil."

"She's not a red devil," Piper says. Piper's been very quiet, more quiet than usual. I hope she'll say what I'm thinking: This slam book sounds pretty mean.

Piper knows what it's like to be on the wrong side of mean. She used to be banned from the Ferguson house in no uncertain terms. It's only recently Bernadette's mom decided to make an exception for her. Piper's Lutheran. Not being able to visit Bernadette's house with the rest of us used to make Piper cry.

"A red devil is a Chinese communist. I don't know what Inga is, but she's definitely not Chinese," says Piper.

"She's German. A germ. She might be contagious, and if she is, you know who's going to catch her disease, don't you?" Mary Virginia points at me.

"Stop that," Jodi says. "Marjorie didn't do anything. Kirk made them sit together."

"All the questions in the slam book have to be about Inga. That's the whole point. That's a good question, though. Write that one down." Bernadette passes a pen to Piper.

"Is Inga Chinese? That's ridiculous."

"No, silly. What is she? Is she Canadian? Is she a germ? Is

she Looney Tunes? You can ask whatever you want."

And then Piper whispers the question everybody wonders, "Is she a Nazi?"

"My dad says that not all the Germans were Nazis," I say quickly. When everyone else just looks at me, I add, "And he should know."

"Not all the Japanese were out to get us, either, but the government locked them up all the same," Jodi says. "I read about it in *Look* magazine. They sent all the Japanese to live in these camps after Pearl Harbor, even if they were living here for their whole lives."

"Like concentration camps?" asks Piper.

"Not like concentration camps. Don't be silly. Americans don't have concentration camps. They were just camps with food and stuff," Jodi says.

"Nazis invented concentration camps, Piper. Don't be a dolt. And I think finding out what kind of Nazi Inga is, well, I think that's pretty important, don't you? Write your question down." Bernadette points to the slam book.

"I can't write that down," Piper says. "What if she sees it?"

"That's the whole point. Maybe she *will* see it and then she'll start to get it."

"Get what?" I ask. My face is in a frown. I can feel it. I don't like this slam book idea one bit.

"Get that she doesn't fit in. That she's not like the rest of us, and she better either do something about it or just go back to where she came from, because we don't like her the way that she is. Who wants to go first?" Piper doesn't take the pen from Bernadette.

"I will," Mary Virginia says.

"What are you going to write?" asks Jodi, leaning in to watch.

"None of your beeswax. You can see when I'm done. Do I have to sign my name?"

Bernadette shakes her head no. "It's secret *and* it's anonymous. So you can be really honest."

"It's not honest to say that she's a germ or that she has horns," I say. If someone wrote that about me and I saw it, I would never come to school again. I remember the look on Inga's face when those boys pushed her mom and told her they didn't want her here. When they called her a DP. I remember how water puddled in the corners of Inga's eyes and her shoulders hunched up to protect her ears. I imagine Inga's reaction as she sees the words in this spiral, worse words written in black and white. Then I imagine her turning to me and asking, "What is horns?"

The imagining makes my eyes burn and my teeth ache.

"It's honest to say that she *acts* like she has horns, or that you *think* that she has horns," says Bernadette, laying lots of emphasis on certain words. And then she adds, talking like a patient teacher, "Margie, you can't be a baby about these things, or you will never survive in junior high. I'm just trying to help you prepare yourself, so you're not so hopeless." Bernadette doesn't bother to pat me on the head like a two-year-old, but that's how I feel.

"And this could be really helpful to Inga, when you think

173

about it. It's just, the truth hurts sometimes." Bernadette passes the spiral and the pen to Mary Virginia. "Okay, you first."

As Mary Virginia takes the book, everyone's eyes peek forward to see what she's going to write.

"No fair," proclaims Bernadette. "It's anonymous, remember? No one's supposed to know who says what. Oh, I almost forgot." She rips a page out of the spiral notebook and writes in big, loopy letters across the top: *Loyalty Oath*. And then she signs her name.

"Here." Bernadette holds the paper out in front of her. "Everybody has to sign this."

"I thought it was anonymous," I say. This whole thing is making me itchy. I pinch my lips together.

"I will keep the piece of paper someplace safe. Only we will know who signed it."

"What does that mean?" asks Piper, tipping her head to read the paper. "'Loyalty Oath.' What's that?"

"It means we won't be commies or undermine the government," I say.

"Don't be a dip brain, Marjorie. A loyalty oath means you will be loyal to whoever asks. Sign this paper and it means you will be loyal to your friends and no one else. Particularly enemies of your friends." She taps the pencil on the paper twice. "And you will not tell who wrote in this slam book, even if they put you in front of a firing squad."

"You going to write all that down? 'Cause I don't want to sign anything unless I know the fine print." Mary Virginia folds her arms.

"That is the fine print. And as long as we are in agreement, we don't have to write it down. Just sign our names. Agreed?" Bernadette looks straight at me. No one else, just me.

"What are you looking at?" I ask.

"Well, you're the only one who's really talked to the enemy, Marjorie. We just need to be sure whose side you're on."

"I didn't know there were sides when I talked to her," I say. I'm mad, but the words come out kind of whiny.

"Well, there are. And you're either on our side or you're on the side of the enemy." Bernadette puts the paper on the floor in front of my folded knees. Then she puts the pen down carefully, like she's trying to make it float. Silence eats up the rest of the room.

I only hesitate for a second before I snatch up the pen and paper. "Okay, but I think this is really dumb. I just want to say that. I've been friends with you guys since forever, and . . ." I scribble my name on the page and put a period at the end. "And I shouldn't have to sign a dumb piece of paper to prove it. There."

I slap the paper back down on the floor in the circle of our knees. One by one, Mary Virginia, Piper, and Jodi sign. Bernadette folds the paper in half. "Good, now we have this just in case."

In case of what? I want to scream. *Why do we all have to sign a stupid paper saying we will be friends with our friends? And why does Bernadette get to keep the piece of paper?* I swallow my questions.

"You can write in the slam book at home and bring it to school on Monday and then we can pass it around. Only we'll have to be really careful so that Kirk the Jerk doesn't snatch it away." Bernadette stands up and opens the top drawer of her dresser, slides the paper in the front and thumps it shut like she's closing a safe instead of her sock drawer.

As we settle into our blankets and sleeping bags on the floor of Bernadette's bedroom, Jodi says, "I hope tomorrow is just like today."

"Tomorrow's Saturday," Mary Virginia points out. "No school."

"No, I mean, I hope nothing happens. Like, I hope the snow and ice don't make the lights go out." Jodi leans back on her pillow. "I definitely hope that stupid siren doesn't go off and blow our ears out again anytime soon."

"That only happens on school days," Bernadette says.

"That's a relief," Mary Virginia says. "At least we know that if the commies are going to drop an H-bomb and evaporate us, it won't happen on a Saturday."

"Mary Virginia, don't talk like that," says Piper.

"Hey, it's 1954, haven't you heard? We only have weekday wars now, weekends off." Mary Virginia laughs. The rest of us kind of chuckle along, not really sure if it's okay to laugh about something as serious as the H-bomb.

"I hope there's never another big war," says Jodi. "Seriously. I just want things to stay, I don't know, even. Forever."

"Oh, don't be a drag. You want things to change. Are you kidding? I mean you want to grow up, don't you? You don't want your mother to be telling you to make your bed and brush your teeth for the rest of your life, do you?" Mary Virginia asks.

"I don't know what I'll do when I grow up anyway," says Jodi. "What do you want to do when you grow up?" We are talking in total darkness, but I can tell she's turned her head and is pointing her question at me.

The truth is, I never think about what I want to do when I grow up. I have never been exactly certain I will grow up. Sometimes I think the world could erupt any minute, just like Owen's volcano, with sparks flying everywhere. They say when the A-bomb went off in Japan, it melted people's skin off and their faces dripped on the ground. I am not sure what the difference is between an A-bomb and an H-bomb, only that the H kind is supposed to be worse. How can something be worse than that?

"That's easy," says Bernadette. "You want to grow up and get married in a white dress and have four perfect babies. A perfect husband who goes to work every day and comes home every night for dinner and a cocktail. It's what every girl wants."

"Four babies?" asks Mary Virginia.

"That's the perfect number, family of six. Any more than that and you won't fit into a station wagon."

"I think I might want to be a doctor," I hear myself say. The fact is, I have never thought about being a doctor until that very moment. Something about Bernadette laying out my life plan for me made that thought just pop out of my mouth.

"Really?" Jodi says. "If you're a doctor, I can bring my babies to you when they're sick."

"If we have a chance to grow up," Piper says, "I'm not even sure I want to bring a baby into a world with the Bomb in it." Everyone knows that Piper is a worrier. She wears it on her face. She chews her lips until she has a chapped circle around them and bites her nails until they bleed. Sometimes she has to wear gloves in school when her fingers are so bad no one can stand to look at them.

"I know what you mean," Jodi says. "My mom says you never know if the wrong somebody is going to push the button, and then we'll all be fried like chicken in bacon fat." She makes a sizzling noise and we all laugh, only not too hard because what she says could really happen.

"Yeah, well, my mom says I have to practice the piano anyway," Mary Virginia says. "She says if we hear bombers, then I can stop playing scales. Not one minute before." We all bust up laughing over that one.

"Just because your mom went to college, that doesn't mean you have to, Marjorie," Bernadette says. "A woman doesn't have to show off that she's smart, there are other ways of getting what you want, right?" She puts one hand behind her head and strikes a pose. Everyone laughs. Even me.

"Bernadette's not calling your mother a show-off," Jodi whispers. "She's just kidding."

"I heard that!" Bernadette announces. "Margie's mom didn't go to college to be a show-off, she was just keeping busy until the war was over, right? Lots of women did crazy things during the war, like work in factories and drive trucks. But now things are back to normal. Only men can be doctors, Marjorie. Girls can be nurses, teachers, or secretaries, and those are just the poor girls who no one wants anyway."

"Yeah," Piper says. Even though I can't see her in the dark room, I know she's twisting her hair around her finger as she tells us about her Aunt Louise. "She was a nurse in the war and had the idea that she could go to medical school on the GI Bill when she landed back in Toledo, but the school wouldn't let her. They said it wouldn't do for a woman to take a place in the school that a man could have because she'd just drop out eventually anyway to have babies. There's only so much room in those kinds of schools."

Even though Dad likes to tell his joke about Army nurses wanting to steal his boots, I can tell he really liked them. He always smiles when he calls them tough cookies. When I imagine a tough cookie, I think of a woman who smokes cigars and can spit like a baseball player. But being an Army nurse would be like knowing how to drive a tank. What do you do with that experience when the war's over?

"Did she?" I ask. "Did she get married and have babies?"

"Nah. She takes tickets at the movie theater in Toledo now. When we go there, she lets us in for free."

"Free popcorn, too?" Jodi asks.

"All you can eat."

"Let's go!" Jodi says. "We could watch movies all the time and not think about anything."

"Yeah, right now," Mary Virginia says. "Grab your dad's car keys, Bernadette. We'll be back by morning, no one will even know." We all laugh, and say, "You first," but no one moves, and we snuggle deeper into our covers. Even though there's a rolled-up towel on the window, we can still feel a breath of cold coming through when the wind gusts and blows.

In the quiet that surrounds us, my mind is carried away with the image of Frank on his motorbike trying to steer through the snow and wind outside. Where is he going to stay when he reaches the prison in Jackson? They aren't going to let him see his brother. He's going to have to wait until visiting hours on Saturday. He should have just let Dad drive him like he did at Christmas. He should have stayed home on a night like this.

Mostly, I think he should not have jammed his greasy, stupid head under my bed and put his grubby hands in that box of books, and if he crashes that stupid bike of his in this snowstorm, it's his own stupid fault. But Mom is going to kill me. And then she's going to be arrested. I think about her being led off in that ugly pink bathrobe, flapping around for all the neighbors to see. I imagine Carol Anne screaming and kicking. That makes me think about whacking Frank in his sleep with the coal shovel that leans up against the furnace. I think I could get in at least two good whacks before he murdered me.

I pull my hands into fists and tell myself not to imagine things that haven't happened yet. That works for about half a minute and then my mind takes off again.

I wish I had said something to Mom about Frank and the books. Bernadette's right. My mom is smart. She could have thought of something. The box of books is important, but is it as important as a boy falling off his motorcycle in a snowstorm and freezing to death in a ditch?

I remember the look on Mrs. Kirk's face when she had Owen by the collar. "Kids burn," she'd told him. I shrink a little when I also remember how she told me, "You're nothing."

I never saw a kid burn, but I expect she's right. But kids can also freeze. Even big kids who act tough in their leather jackets.

The inside of my head is swirling, echoing the storm outside, and suddenly lightning flashes in my brain.

I stand straight up. "I need to use the phone," I say.

"It's eleven-thirty. Your parents are in bed. Go to sleep," Bernadette says.

"I'll be right back." I step over sleeping bodies and race for the phone in the kitchen.

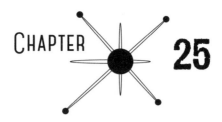

CHAPTER 25

On Saturday morning after the sleepover, Mom tells me it's good that I called because it gave Dad a chance to put his pants on before the Michigan State Patrolman rang the doorbell. Frank had hit a patch of black ice on the highway and laid the bike on its side, skidding under an eighteen-wheeler.

"The only reason he wasn't torn up worse than he was is because he was wearing his pop's padded hunting overalls and that dreadful black leather jacket," says Mom. She doesn't ask why I didn't call them earlier. I had maybe lied a little and told Dad he better check Frank's bed, that maybe (only maybe) he *might* have gone someplace on his motorcycle and that just *maybe* that someplace was over to the prison in Jackson. But I told him I wasn't sure.

The truth was, I was exactly sure where he had gone.

Dad had followed the patrol car to the hospital where Frank was having his arm set in a cast and his broken collarbone taped up. "They didn't pull in here until after four this morning, so don't go making a lot of noise," Mom says.

"Did he say anything?" I ask. I think about the books. About Frank's threat to tell Dad. I chew on my nail and try to read my mother's face.

I look at her eyes for signs that they've been crying. I look at her mouth to see if it's angry. I look for any sign that someone found a dangerous book in Frank's gym bag when he was scraped up off the highway.

"I think Frank is just grateful to be back home in his own bed. He's beat up pretty badly." Only my mom would say "badly" and not just "beat up pretty bad." She can't be too upset if her grammar's right. "They think they might be able to straighten out the bike." She sighs. "Unfortunately."

"Mom?" I lower my voice to a whisper. "We need to talk about those books under my bed."

"Oh, sweetheart. That's the least of our worries today. Consider those books just parked there till this whole book-banning thing blows over, which it will. Things always do. Don't give it another thought. Oh, don't look at me like that." She wrinkles her nose and makes a bug-eyed face. "You know what Grandma Mona would say."

"Grandma Mona knows about the books?" I gasp.

"Cripes, no. But she'd be quick to tell you if you don't wipe that look off your face, it will stay that way permanently."

"But Mom." I know I am sounding pathetic. I just want the books to be gone. "They can't park there forever."

"Sweetie, when you live as long as I have, you'll learn. Everything passes eventually. This country's survived revolution, a civil war, two world wars; we can survive this Cold War nonsense. Let's just not get arrested in the meantime," she adds in a whisper, finger to her lips. "So mum's the word."

"Mom!" I cry. *Arrested?* I can just imagine what Bernadette would have to say about that. I would be a total goner at school.

183

"Oh, I'm just kidding. Cheer up, sweetie. There's a new baby to celebrate! Forget the books. Here, pick up a towel and help me dry these dishes." Mom, Carol Anne, and I are in the kitchen with the door closed, trying to be quiet.

"Mom," I singsong. "What if we just put them on the doorstep of the library in the middle of the night?" Then I whisper, "*Arrested?*"

"Shh, nobody's going to be arrested. Just stop talking about it. We have enough to worry about right here."

Carol Anne has built another Empire State Building on the floor, this one out of cracker and cereal boxes.

"Neeeeyoowww," she whines as she circles a raisin box around like one of the airplanes sent to shoot at King Kong. She stutters like a machine gun, "Tatatatat." Pretty soon the building topples over and she starts building it again.

Mom has made a pile of cookies for the baby shower later today. I pick up a dish towel to help with the pans.

After a few are passed between us hand to hand, I ask her, "Why did you go to college?"

Mom looks out the window. "I was in college when I met your dad." She stops washing and stares at a place somewhere beyond the Fergusons' backyard. "He was working at the gas station by campus. He wasn't so worried about following all the rules like he is now. I thought he was daring and fun and that he looked just like Frank Sinatra. So, we were married and had you. I had to drop out, of course." She sloshes some rinse water onto the dish rack. "When he volunteered for the army and went away, I moved back in with my parents, Grandpa Henry and Grandma

Ethel. Grandpa Henry told me to go back and finish, so I did."

"Yeah, but why did you go in the first place? Did you want to be a doctor or something?" Mom's washing and passing me bowls one at a time.

"I didn't think that far ahead, I guess. It was Grandpa Henry's dream for me to be the first one in the family to go to college. Grandpa Henry could be very convincing." She looks at me.

"You don't remember my father at all, I don't expect." I shake my head. "Such a shame. You were only a baby when we lived with him. He was the kindest man in the world. He only had a barbershop in Zanesville, Ohio, but everyone treated him like he was the mayor of Main Street. When the war came around, he was too old to serve. He did his duty by being on the draft board. All the boys had a number, and they'd draw the numbers out in Washington and send them to the local draft boards. The draft boards would meet and announce who was going to go. At first they had some say in the matter. They could offer some of the boys deferments. The board would balance it against how many boys that family had sent already and how many they could still keep on the farms. Raising food was considered war work at first. Every time after they made up the list of who'd be drafted next, he'd come home, sit at the kitchen table, and just cry."

She's using a steel wool pad and scrubbing hard on a pan that looks clean to me. "By the end of the war, they were taking anybody who had a pulse. Daddy even tried to volunteer. 'Wherever you have men, you need a barber,' he said. But he was almost sixty years old, and they wouldn't take him. The war broke him.

"It also fell to the draft board to put the notices in the paper of the boys who weren't coming home, boys he felt like he'd sent to their deaths. He died of a broken heart—just before the armistice."

"Here," I say and reach for the scratched-up pan so she can start on the next one.

"Just let me get this little bit here." And she scrubs at a spot I can't see.

"I thought all the GIs just signed up to go fight the Nazis like Dad did."

She finally finishes with the pan and passes it under the rinse water. "A lot of those Ohio farm boys were from German stock. Others had the view that the Europeans had been fighting among themselves for centuries and that's why they'd come to America, to put all the fighting behind them and start over. The Italians hated the Irish, the Irish hated the English, the English hated the French, and everyone hated the Russians. Everybody who pulls up stakes to come to America comes here because they hate someone. Some of those men, or maybe I should say the mothers of some of those young men, needed convincing that we are all on the same team. That's what the draft board was all about."

"Grandma Mona hates the Catholics," I say.

Mom laughs and kisses me on the top of the head, "That's a whole other layer of hatred, pumpkin. Grandma Mona's not only a Presbyterian; she's a stubborn Scottish Presbyterian. I'm afraid there's no talking her out of that one."

Bing bong. The doorbell. Mom and I bolt for the door before the bell rings again and wakes up Dad. Standing on the porch

186

are Inga and her mom. I look at Inga just long enough to know it's her. I don't look her in the face. Mom invites them in, but Inga shakes her head. She holds out a pair of blue, knitted baby booties stuffed with cotton balls. "For the baby party," she says.

Mom's holding the door open like she doesn't care that she's trying to heat the whole outdoors, which is what she tells me if I keep the door open one second in this weather.

"Won't your mother come to the baby shower?" Mom asks Inga. Then she looks at Mrs. Scholtz and says, "Please come."

Inga answers in what sounds like a rehearsed speech. "My mother is very pleased to be invited, but she is having to work today. You will let the mother know that she wishes the new baby a long and happy life." When she finishes, Mrs. Scholtz, who's been watching Inga's every word, looks at Mom and smiles.

"Well, yes," Mom says. She's trying to hold the door open and take the gift while reaching out to shake hands with Mrs. Scholtz. "Another time, then, tell her." Inga nods.

As soon as the door closes, I dart to the front window and stand behind the curtain where I can't be seen. I watch them walking away hand in hand. I imagine this will wind up as a question in the slam book: *Why does Inga hold hands with her mother like a baby?*

"Look at these," Mom says, leaning against the front door. "She must have stayed up all night knitting these little booties. Aren't they just the sweetest things you have ever seen?"

Actually, the booties look to be the exact same color as Inga's too-small sweater that's been itching my arm every day at school. I can tell because they are the same sky color as her eyes.

"The baby's going to kick those scratchy things off in two seconds," I say, peeking between the wall and the curtain.

"Marjorie, what is wrong with you?" Mom looks at me like I just bit the head off a chicken. "These are the most darling little booties I've ever seen."

"They're scratchy. Trust me," I mumble as I edge the curtain over to widen my view out the window, trying not to be seen from the street.

"Are you hiding from that girl, Inga? You're acting ridiculous." She whips the curtains back. "That's enough of that."

I drop to a crouch and stare down at my stocking feet. "Mom!" I screech. "What are you doing?"

"What are *you* doing?" she asks, looking down at me. "I thought you were friends with her."

"No! I mean, not really. It's just, you know . . . she's so different." I peek over the windowsill just in time to see them turn the corner.

"Up off your knees, young lady." Mom grabs me by the sleeve. "Up!" I stumble to my feet; glad to see that Inga and her mother are out of sight. "You listen to me. *Different's* what we all are. Or what we should be." Mom looks at the ceiling. We can hear Dad moving in their bedroom over our heads. She puts her hands on both of my shoulders, the blue booties scratching my ear. I must be growing taller, because she doesn't even have to bend over to look me straight in the face.

She talks fast, "You asked me why I went to college and the answer is because Grandpa Henry told me to go. But you didn't

188

ask me what I learned there. I learned this: Books, like the books upstairs, they stretch your brain, so there's enough room for lots of ideas: good ideas, bad ideas, ideas different than the ideas you grow up with. From those ideas you can make your own ideas, different ideas. Different is a good way to be. Don't let anyone tell you otherwise. When people try too hard to be the same, that's when the shooting starts."

"What kind of conspiracy are you two cooking up?" Dad asks as he clomps down the steps.

"Wouldn't you like to know," says Mom playfully. "Our lips are sealed." Dad grabs the dish towel out of my hand and snaps it in Mom's direction.

"I haff vays of making you talk," he teases with a fake accent. She pretends to run, and he chases her, but she lets herself get caught in his long spider arms.

I love Dad when he's like this. Fun and playful instead of dark-eyed and strict. I remember what Frank said about his pop, that he was different before the war. Was Dad different when Mom first met him? Did he like to goof around when he worked at the gas station? He probably wasn't as worried about losing that job as he is about losing his job at Chrysler, since he didn't have me or Carol Anne to worry about back then. Maybe becoming strict is just something that naturally happens to grown-ups, like gray hair or wanting coffee in the morning instead of orange juice.

Back then, he probably didn't jump out of his chair like he was being shot from a cannon, or holler out loud in the middle of the night. His gums probably didn't bleed, and his feet probably didn't peel in cold weather. But was he a different person?

I look hard at him.

I don't see any part of him that looks like Frank Sinatra.

Like magic, Carol Anne appears and jumps into Dad's arms and curls up like a boiled macaroni noodle. "How's my little baby girl?" he asks.

"Look what that Mrs. Scholtz brought over for Lydia's and George's new baby. I'm sure she knitted them herself," says Mom.

"How about that," Dad says, not even looking at the booties and putting Carol Anne back on the ground gently. "She coming to your little shindig?"

"No, we tried to talk her into it, didn't we, Marjorie?" Mom squints at me and I kind of smile. "It's maybe good she said no. Viola Fisher accepted the invitation to come and I don't know how she would take it, you know." She looks from me to Dad. "Which is not to say that you shouldn't be nice to that girl in school, do you hear me? It's not like she started the war."

"Yes, but—"

"Listen to your mother," Dad says. He opens the door to the basement and calls down the stairs to Frank, "Don't you know people die in bed?"

"Go easy on the boy. He's so banged up," Mom says to Dad in a loud whisper.

"Frank, you hearing me? Use your good arm to throw a shovel of coal in the furnace and report topside for duty."

He closes the door again and faces Mom. "Boy's keeping us up all night, he's got to pay the piper. I'm thinking of a whole list of one-armed chores for him today. Gonna build his intestinal fortitude."

"I guess," says Mom. "Cripes, it's late. The shower is in less than an hour. Don't be too harsh."

"World's a harsh place, Lila. Boy's got a lot more tearing at him than a broken arm. His pop's gone, brother's in the clink, and Frank, he doesn't have it so bad, living here. He's got him a case of survivor's guilt. Seen it plenty of times in boys not much older than he is. Best thing he can do is get up and get on with it."

"I suppose," Mom answers, starting to climb the stairs. "C'mon, Carol Anne. Help your Mama dress," she says, as if there were any chance in the world Carol Anne would let her go upstairs alone.

"I thought Frank was worried about Charles," I say.

"Charles is just fine," Dad says. "With good behavior, he'll be out come fall and he'll have a high school diploma and hopefully enough sense to never go joyriding in a stolen car again. So tell me something, you say this Scholtz family moved here from Canada?" The question's directed at me.

"Yeah," I answer. "Inga speaks French and everything," I add quickly.

"She speaks German, too, right?"

I'm not sure what he wants me to say. If I say they are German, is that going to make him mad? "I never really heard her talking German," I lie, my words coming out like I spread peanut butter on graham crackers, slowly, carefully.

"Don't be thinking you need to protect anybody by telling

me stories, Marjorie. They speak German, right? That's what the mother speaks, am I right?"

I look to where Mom was standing for help, but she's disappeared upstairs.

I nod and shrug, not wanting to lie, but not wanting to whip the curtain back on the whole truth either.

Dad nods back and kind of purses his lips together. I can't tell if it's a mad look or not. I watch him carefully.

"You ever meet a Mr. Scholtz?" Dad asks me.

I shake my head no. It's true I never met him. I don't tell Dad that I think I saw him that once watching us play Nazis. I don't tell him that I met his cap. The black cap with the button on top. The cap on the hook in Inga's house.

"Mmm," Dad says. "German, eh? I wonder what he did in the war."

This is the question that comes up whenever one of my friends' fathers is mentioned. Or any man, really. What did he do in the war? Pacific or Europe? Army? Navy? Marines? Did he see real combat or was he a pencil pusher? Was he 4-F? And if he was, he better be blind or at least missing one eyeball. Flat feet was no reason to stay home when so many went off to be killed.

I know that Piper's dad joined up for pilot training before our country even entered the war. He served under MacArthur and flew airplanes that picked up stranded sailors in the Pacific. He named her after a plane he trained on called the Piper Cub. And Mary Virginia's dad had to hide in a barn in France for two weeks after he parachuted into the wrong place. Owen's dad was in the Pacific; Jodi's dad was in Europe. It's just something people ask about dads. But this is the first time I ever thought about a man who might have fought for the other side.

I shrug. This conversation makes me want to bolt. It's already lasted at least two sentences longer than a normal conversation with Dad. A normal conversation goes like this, "You done your homework, Margie-girl?" and I say, "Yes," and he says, "Good girl." Or I say, "Not yet," and he says, "Get busy."

"I might have to meet this Scholtz," Dad says, shoving his hands in his pockets.

"You can't," I blurt. My mind races. "I mean, they don't have a phone."

"Well, good thing I got feet then, isn't it? You know where they live, right? Maybe you can walk me over there sometime this week."

Why does Marjorie visit the Scholtz house after school?

Is it true that Marjorie is friends with a germ?

Why does Marjorie's father want to talk to a Nazi?

I can see a slam book with my name on it. If I go over to the Scholtz house again, my friends are going to have questions. Big questions. Questions I don't want to read about in a book passed around at school.

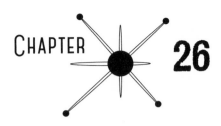

CHAPTER 26

I help Mom to the car with her cookies and gifts for the baby. Dad has lured Carol Anne out to the garage so Mom can make her escape in peace. "Careful," Mom says as I pick up a tray of little sandwiches.

A baby shower is not exactly a sleepover with pillows and records, but it's easy to see that Mom's planning to have a good time with her friends. I stand at the door and wave as she pulls out of the drive.

When I turn around, I come face to face with red and purple and white.

Frank. His face looks like it's been ripped off and painted back on in bright colors. His arm is in a sling, and a giant white pad the size of a slice of bread covers one ear.

I gasp, one hand flying up to my mouth.

"Thanks, punk," he hisses through puffed-up lips. There are black stitches marching straight out of one side of his mouth.

"Kind of hard not to notice," I say.

"I almost made it, ya know."

"Almost made it to heaven?" I say. And then because he looks pretty pathetic, "Sorry."

"Yeah, I'll bet."

"Okay, you two." It's Dad. He and Carol Anne are both wearing their coats.

"How 'bout we all take a walk up to the gas station for a little consultation on where to start straightening out that bike?"

Frank and I both stand there. For once we have found something we have in common. Neither one of us wants to go anywhere.

"That gas tank's gonna take some welding and that's beyond me," Dad says. He lays a hand on Frank's good shoulder. Frank winces. He must hurt all over.

I have zero interest in standing around staring at tools and tires at the gas station while he talks to some guy I don't know about motorcycle repairs I don't care about.

"Come on, it's not that bad of a day. Let's take a walk. Go out and blow the stink off."

Funny Dad should say that since I think gas stations rank right up there with dirty diaper pails and open sewers as places full of stink.

The phone rings. "Now who could that be?" asks Dad. He motions to Frank to put his coat on as he strides over to pick up the receiver.

As soon as he says, "Yep, she's right here," I know I'm off the hook. I practically skip to the phone.

"Hi, it's Piper."

"Oh, hi," I say. "Just a minute." I cover the mouthpiece and negotiate with Dad, who says I can stay home as long as I don't burn the house down.

That's twice in two days I've been warned to not burn a place down. I want to ask if I look like an arsonist, but instead I just say, "I'm just going to talk to Piper and then take a nap, Dad. You guys go ahead."

"I'm gonna beg off, too. I didn't sleep so good last night." Frank turns to retreat to his basement lair. The door closes behind him.

"You need to learn to sleep no matter what." Dad yells after him. "And that goes for you, too," he says to me.

"Okay, Dad." I nod, my hand over the telephone receiver.

"Got to be battle ready."

"Right." I turn back to the phone.

"Looks like it's just you and me, sweet pea." Dad takes Carol Anne's hand in his and they head for the door. She's jumping for joy to be going on a walk with Dad because she's too young to know how boring gas stations are. I settle into the chair by the telephone table.

"I'm back."

"It's Piper."

"I know, you said that already."

The phone is silent, and I can picture Piper chewing on her lip on the other end. "You okay?" I ask.

Another few seconds of silence.

"Bernadette's mad at me."

Bernadette, mad? Only a few hours ago the slumber party had ended, and we were all laughing and waving good-bye. "Don't be silly, Piper. You worry too much."

"Don't laugh, Marjorie. Mary Virginia wrote her part in the slam book before we left Bernadette's and I'm next and I forgot to bring the book home with me and Bernadette called and I'm really in trouble. She says I don't think the slam book is important, and that's not true. I do think it's important, I really, really do."

"Sure you do, Piper. Don't sweat it. Bernadette's not mad."

"Do you know that for sure? Have you talked to her?" Her voice is urgent. It's as if she's telling me there's a train coming and we better get off the tracks.

"No, I haven't talked to her, but it's not that big of a deal."

"Oh, yes, Marjorie. It *is* a big deal. It's a very big deal. I might be banned from her house again or worse."

"Why don't you have your mother ban Bernadette from your house, then you'll be even." I'm not sure what the problem is between the Lutherans and the Catholics, but I know it goes both ways.

"My mother *did* ban her from my house, it's just nobody cares what I do or my mom does. Everybody just cares about Bernadette. And she's made us all sign that loyalty oath. This is really serious. What if she starts a slam book about me? If she did, I'd just die. Please. You have to talk to her for me. You know her best."

I manage to calm Piper down, as much as she can be calmed down. Piper's like a kite string on a windy day most of the time, ready to snap any second. I promise to call Bernadette and tell her that Piper thinks the slam book is important. I decide not to tell Piper that I've been worried about the same thing. This slam book idea could be turned against anyone.

After I hang up, I run up the stairs and flop on my bed, but I'm way too worked up to take a nap. I'm not sleepy tired. I'm fed-up tired. I roll over and slam my fist into my pillow once for Kirk making Inga sit next to me in the first place. I slam it again for Inga. And again for *Curious George*. And twice for Frank. I raise my fist again for the box of books hidden under my bed, but my hand stops in midair as I realize I am home alone. Well, as good as alone. Frank is two floors away.

I slip off the bed and pull my box of National Geographic maps and travel folders out into the middle of the floor. Flat on my belly on the floor, I can barely reach the box of books that Mom jammed under there. She may be right that books stretch the brain, but, trying to move a box of them with my fingertips, I quickly discover they are more likely to stretch my arm out of its socket. I roll over on my back and use my feet to pull the box towards me. Right on top sits the *1984* book that landed me in trouble at the library. I pick it up, slip it under my pillow, and quickly push the box back, shoving it all the way against the wall with both feet.

Why is Marjorie an instigator?

Is Marjorie a commie sympathizer?

Questions crowd my brain as I open *1984* and begin to read about what happens to this guy Winston. People are always watching him, too. Only this story is set in the future where they have more ways to watch him. The watchers are also mind-readers, so he has to hide in the corner of his room where no one can see him think. The Thought Police hover outside of his window in helicopters, and bombs go off every day. In a weird way, at first this makes me feel a little bit better. At least my life isn't as bad as his. But it also puts me on high alert, like hearing about a robbery in another town. I hurry to the window and pull down the shade, just to be on the safe side.

The book has lots of words I never saw before. Some of them, like the word *truncheon*, I just skip over and figure I can understand the story whether I know that word or not. Other strange words just explain themselves, like *Newspeak*. It's an invented language they speak in Oceania, the made-up country where Winston lives. It's kind of an upside-down language where *war* means *peace* and *freedom* means *slavery*. I am only on page six of this book when it really starts to turn scary. The Thought Police are everywhere, watching him all the time. Even Winston's TV set can read his mind, so he has to wear a fake smile in order to watch the news and not be in trouble. He takes a big risk and buys a blank book that he wants to use for a diary. Writing thoughts in a diary is so illegal it could get him sent to a horrible prison with no windows and lots of barbed wire, which (according to Newspeak) is run by the Ministry of Love.

I can't see into the future as far as 1984, but I can see what's going to happen in this book. This guy Winston's going to wind up in big trouble for thought crimes, and it's not going to have a happy ending. I close the book and put it back under my pillow. I'm in no mood for unhappy endings, and reading this book is like pulling a heavy load of bricks in a wagon. Not easy.

Since *1984* takes place in London, I decide to pull out a map of England. I kneel beside my collection of brochures and pull out one with Big Ben, this huge clock tower, on the cover. *LONDON!* it says in blue and red.

"We're back," Dad announces as he slaps open the door. I jump and fall backwards like someone's pulled the rug out from under my knees.

"Hey, kid. Don't look so spooked. What are you doing with the shades down? Beautiful day outside." He walks over and releases the shade so it snaps up loud as a gunshot. I jump again. Carol Anne scampers into the room.

"Can I see? Can I see?" She plops down beside my box and starts grabbing at things. Instinctively, I cover it with both arms. My heart's racing like a revved-up car. I can hardly breathe.

"What ya got there? Ahhhh. Beautiful town, London. Hope you see it someday. Hope you see all the places in that box. Changes who you are, I can tell you that." Dad hangs over the box for a second. I glance nervously to the side and see the corner of *1984* sticking out from under my pillow. My ears pound.

"You think you could be a good big sister and watch Carol Anne until your mother's home? Shouldn't be too long. I'm going to roust Frank and take him out to kick tires on some used cars. See if we can wrap a little more metal around him with some of the money his dad left him. Looks like repairing that bike might just be throwing good money after bad."

I am panting like I'm sinking in the deep end.

"Calm down, kid. A little gun-shy, there, eh?" Dad scrubs the top of my head with his hard hand.

I nod. There's still not enough breath in me to speak.

"We'll be back before supper. Tell your mom." He turns around as he's about to leave, "Hey, get a load a this. Guess who's moonlighting as a weekend mechanic up to the gas station? German, name a Scholtz. Turns out he was a tank mechanic in the war, and guess what else?"

I'm not even blinking, I'm listening so hard. "What?" I mouth the word.

"He has a kid named Inga! Your friend's dad, working up to the gas station, what do you make of that? I invited him over for a cup a joe next weekend. Maybe a beer. Who knows? See what he's all about. Oh, and I invited Inga to come with him."

"Frank," is all I say. Kind of to myself and kind of out loud. Frank is going to go off like a box of screaming fireworks if Mr. Scholtz comes over. And it's not the best time for a visit from Inga, either.

"Frank'll deal with it. Don't set the house on fire. Be back in an hour."

Dad's out the door and down the stairs before my heart slows to something close to normal. What if I'd had the wrong box pulled out? By the time I come to my senses, Carol Anne has discovered that she can slide on my brochures. She's skating around the room, one foot on Sweden and the other on Cuba.

"Give me those," I yell, snatching back the glossy brochures.

I throw everything in the box any which way and shove it under my bed. "Those are mine. No touching!" The words come out meaner than they need to be, and her lower lip begins to quiver.

"I want Mommy," she cries. She throws her head back, "Mommy!"

"Shh. Shh. Here, you want me to read you *Curious George*?" I offer. I run to her bookshelf and start to pull off all her favorites.

She screams for Mom a few more times, but I wear her down with a stack of books and promises to read every one. Twice. We sit in the same place that I sat with Inga the week before, reading about the man in the yellow hat. The sun comes in, and the room fills with warmth. Carol Anne toots her pretend bugle, just like George in the animal show. Mom comes home before I'm finished with the stack of books and sits down with us on Carol Anne's bed.

"How are my best girls?" she asks, bouncing the bed and making us both giggle like babies, "I am the luckiest mom in the whole wide world, you know that?"

It isn't until after dinner and *The Honeymooners* that I remember the hidden book and reach under my pillow. Its hard cover feels cold against my hand. I wish there were someone I could talk to about this book business. I wish there were someone I could trust, someone who wouldn't tell the police—or worse—Bernadette.

I try and think who that might be. Not Jodi or Piper, and definitely not Mary Virginia, who would tell your deepest secret to an entire assembly of kids if she thought she could wiggle a laugh out of them.

For some reason I can't really explain, I wish I could talk to Inga.

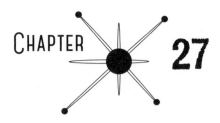

CHAPTER 27

"You signed a loyalty oath. Remember?" Mary Virginia tries to pass me the slam book as we are hanging up our coats on Monday morning. "Here."

"Don't be so pushy," I answer and try to hurry past her to my desk.

Mary Virginia catches me by the arm. "You're with us or you're against us, Marjorie."

"Did Bernadette tell you to say that? She can tell me herself." I jerk my arm away.

"We need to know where you stand. Are you on our side or not?" She pokes me with the slam book, but I refuse to take it. Instead I point to Inga, already at our desk and working on the story problem. Mike is leaning over the aisle, helping her with the words.

"Not now!" I want to scream that I don't want to take sides.

"Okay, I'll give it to Jodi then, but you have to do this, like everyone else." She tips her head. "You gave your word."

"I know. I will." I run to my desk before she has a chance to try and jam the book in my hands again.

The nervousness that Piper was feeling over the weekend is now jumping in my stomach. What if people get bored with writing about Inga? Who will be next?

The last thing in the world I want to do is go sit beside Inga. Still, that's the safest place, because everybody has to be at least a little careful around her, or the whole secret about the slam book will be blown to smithereens.

Inga's leaning over the aisle asking Mike a question and doesn't even look up when I sit down. It's like there's a cold war between us. No bombs. No smiles. Just a frigid silence.

Later that morning, while Mrs. Kirk's writing this week's spelling words on the board with her back turned, I see Jodi pass the slam book to Piper. And then during silent reading, Piper passes it to Gloria Brown.

How did Gloria get in on this?

Pretty soon, it becomes apparent that all the girls are in on the slam book. On her way to the pencil sharpener, Bernadette drops the slam book on my desk. Right under Inga's nose. Luckily, her name is written on the inside. But it's clear to see that someone's drawn a head with braids and horns on the cover.

Quickly as I can, I slip the book into the cubbyhole under my side of the desk.

But Inga sees. She raises one eyebrow.

"It's nothing," I whisper. These are the first words I've said to her in over a week. She just stares at me for a second and turns her eyes back to the board.

Inga's smart. She's going to figure out what's going on in no time, if she hasn't already. And I know at some point, I am not going to be able to duck out of contributing to the slam book. Before recess, I pass the book to Mary Virginia just to be rid of it.

At recess, a group of giggling girls forms behind the school.

They are circled around an open notebook, and I know exactly which one. Are they laughing at what's in the book, or at the fact that I haven't written anything so far?

I decide it's a good day to help Kirk clean erasers and go back inside.

Friday, on our way to school, Bernadette makes a big show of being disgusted with me, huffing and snorting. I want to ask her if she's trying to do an imitation of Ferdinand the Bull or just acting that way by accident.

"What's the matter?" I ask. As if I don't know.

She stops, feet planted. "Look, I know what you're doing."

"What?" I ask, pushing forward, keeping myself focused on not stepping in any puddles from the melting snow.

"You're not writing what you honestly think in the slam book, that's what." Bernadette says. Then she has to rush to catch up to me because I refuse to stop walking just so she can lecture me.

"How do you know?" I ask. "It's anonymous."

"Don't try to be cute. I know your handwriting as well as I know every freckle on your nose, and I went through this book page by page last night, and you haven't written a single question or answer in the whole book. You better write something, or everyone's going to know."

"Know what?" I ask.

"That you're a Nazi lover. Are you dense? I can't protect you from this, Marjorie. You have to do it or people are going to be out for you. Stop being such a fraidy-cat."

I can't think of words to say back. Is that what she really thinks? That I'm a target and she's my defense system? We reach

Billy's busy corner, traffic whizzing by, sending up slush balls. I close my mouth tight, partly because I don't want to make her madder than she already is, but mostly because I don't want to wind up eating gray snow.

"Wait," Billy holds out his arms as we pause for traffic to clear.

"She's not some bird with a broken wing you need to protect, you know." Bernadette hisses at me, "For all we know, her dad ran a concentration camp and her mother was a spy."

"Her mother was not a spy," I say, finding my voice. "That's crazy cakes." I don't mention the black cap I saw hanging on the hook at Inga's house, or how I'm pretty sure it was her dad who was staring at us at the snow fort.

"Maybe you should read the slam book before you stand up for her."

"That stuff's all made up. What am I going to learn from that?"

"You won't know until you read it."

"But none of it's true."

"It's what people believe. That part is true. And she needs to know what people are thinking. The whole point of this slam book is to help her. Do you want to show her how to be a real American or not?"

Before I have a chance to tell her that I don't think made-up questions and answers are going to help anything, Billy puts his arms down and turns to look at us. For an instant our eyes connect.

"Good morning, Billy." Bernadette throws her shiniest smile

in his direction, but he doesn't look at her. He just looks at me. And then barely, just barely, he shakes his head.

Or I think he shakes his head. It looks like a little head shake, but I'm not sure.

We step into the crosswalk. I look over my shoulder at him when we're halfway across the street, but he's busy watching for cars and holding back another group of kids.

"Don't be so obvious," says Bernadette.

"What?"

"Everybody knows you are goners over Billy. Even he knows it. You'll never make anything happen with him until you learn how to play hard to get."

"Did you talk to him about me?" I stop in my footprints.

It's Bernadette's turn to keep on walking. "I didn't have to, silly. It's written all over your face. Hurry up, or we're going to be late." Bernadette keeps talking the rest of the way to school about all the things different girls have written in the book. Questions about Inga's stockings, why her mother picks her up from school every day, and (didn't I see this coming?) how she holds her mother's hand. Bernadette thinks that's hilarious.

"This slam book is really going to help Inga fit in, since she obviously doesn't know how to be an American on her own. But then what can you expect from a DP, anyway? She's going to thank us for this book when we give it to her, you'll see."

I am hardly listening to Bernadette because my thoughts are caught up in a spider web of confusion. What was Billy's little head shake all about? Is Bernadette right? Am I that obvious? Was Billy giving me a signal not to look at him?

Bernadette just keeps quoting things from the book and explaining who wrote what. Clearly there is nothing anonymous about any of it. Finally, after I've been silent for a whole block, she asks, "Why's your face all squinched up like that?"

"It's cold," I answer.

"Liar." Bernadette says, pulling her mouth to one side. "Sometimes I wonder if you and I even speak the same language. You're so dense."

Bernadette's right. No way are we speaking the same language if she thinks a spiral full of mean questions translates into being helpful. Am I supposed to believe that if the slam book hurts Inga a lot, that means she'll be helped even more? What kind of language is that?

"Newspeak." The word just pops out of my mouth.

"What's that?"

"Nothing."

"You better get with it, Margie. Nobody likes a stick in the mud. Remember that." And right before we walk into school, she lifts my mittened hand up and puts the book in it. "It's your turn."

I jam the book into my cubby and take out a piece of paper, but as hard as I try, I cannot make sense out of the morning math problem. The words are swimming in circles, doing a water ballet on the board.

Maybe Billy was just looking into space, and I walked in the way of his eyes. Did he hear us talking about the slam book? Does he know what it's for?

"Marjorie? Would you like to come to the board and write the answer to this morning's word problem? No? I didn't think so. Extract your head from the clouds, Miss Campbell, and focus on your schoolwork. Who can help me out here?"

I feel Inga's hand shoot into the air.

"Miss Scholtz? Well, well. Let's see what you have, dear." Inga stands tall when I let her out of the desk. As she walks to the board, I can hear snickering behind me, and I know she must hear it, too. But that doesn't keep her from writing the right answer on the board. "Very good, Miss Scholtz. Maybe a little of your perseverance will rub off on your desk mate."

At that moment, I am tempted to whip out the slam book and write, *Why is Inga such a show off?* But I don't.

At the end of the day, I still haven't written anything. I lie and tell Bernadette that I have to take Carol Anne to her friend's house and that we can't walk home together.

"Where's the slam book?" is all Bernadette wants to know.

"I have it in my book bag," I say. "I'll work on it over the weekend."

"Yes, you will," she says, and runs off to join Mary Virginia and Piper.

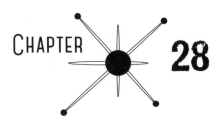

Chapter 28

"Ouch," I say, looking at Frank's still beat-up face as he sits down across the table from me. It's not time for dinner yet and we are both just in from school.

There hasn't been that much improvement in Frank's face in a week. His left eye has faded from red-purple to a sick shade of orange-purple. The huge bandage has shrunk to a piece of adhesive tape with scabs and stitching growing out of it. His arm is in a sling and his shirt won't quite button because of all the bandages on his chest.

"It's not as bad as it looks," he says, wincing as he slumps into a dining room chair. "Want to feel how my ribs shift when I move?"

"No." I don't want to touch Frank ever in my entire life, let alone feel his broken ribs.

Dad let him stay home on Monday and Tuesday, but the rest of this week he's been at school, though I don't know why. He can't carry books or hold a pencil. Dad says it's his responsibility to make sure that Frank graduates. "After you get the piece of paper," Dad says, "you can do as you please."

"Come on now." Frank gently touches his shirt. "Girls at school can't get enough of it. I got them running their hands up and down my side in every class."

"Right," I say. My book bag's splattered open on the table, the contents sliding out. I'm supposed to be reading the chapter on Ancient Rome in my social studies book, but decide to have some graham crackers and peanut butter first. Frank and I sit looking at each other.

"Hope I'm not interrupting anything too interesting." Frank smiles as he glances at what I'm reading.

"Not really." I have four squares of graham crackers counted out, and peanut butter spread all the way to the edges, exactly the way I like them.

"What you got here?" Frank reaches up with his good arm and pulls at the slam book, which is now covered with drawings and doodles, pictures supposed to represent Inga. In big red letters it says, *Go Home.*

I try to pull it toward me, but it sticks underneath his fingers.

"Man, you girls start early on this stuff, don't ya?" He pulls his hand back.

"What stuff?" I jam the spiral notebook back in my shoulder bag, but it doesn't want to stay inside.

"You know, boys'll pound on each other, but I swear, girls are nastier."

Surprised? Angry? Invaded? I am not sure how to feel about Frank looking at the stuff in my book bag and at the slam book, even from the outside. Mostly, I feel embarrassed.

"It's not mine."

"Never is. Those things belong to no one and everyone at the same time. I wasn't born yesterday, you know."

In a few months, Frank will graduate and be out of my life. He's supposed to go in the army. Or maybe the Marines. He hasn't decided, but he can't stand the thought of being cooped up on a ship for months, so the navy's out. Looking at him all bashed up, he doesn't look like he's old enough to be a GI. He looks like a little boy with messed-up hair and a boo-boo. He licks his lips and closes his eyes, letting out a small moan.

"You okay?" I ask.

"Will be, I guess. Nothing that won't heal. Guess I'm better off than whoever that book is for."

"Ugh," I groan and rest my head on my hand. "I have to think of something to write in there, and I don't want to."

"Have to?"

"Well, I'm supposed to. Everyone else did. It's my turn."

"Next there might be one a these with your name on it." Frank taps the book with one finger.

My worst nightmare. Wide eyes betray my horror.

"Relax. I'm just saying that's how these things work. It's an intimidation game. You don't have to play, ya know."

"I really don't want to hurt her feelings." I don't stop to tell Frank he's defending the Kraut girl who had him all upset.

"This isn't about some other girl. This is about you, see? Whoever started this is trying to control you. Control all of yous. You gonna let that happen?"

"But everybody . . . I don't know." I'm nibbling my graham cracker into smaller and smaller pieces and licking my finger to collect the crumbs.

"Sure, you do. You know. Evil is as evil does. Don't matter if everybody else is doing it. Like your dad says, right is right and wrong is—"

"Wrong is nobody, I know." Dad's been telling me that for as long as I can remember. "You think slam books are evil?"

"Don't you?"

"I don't know."

"Yes, you *do*."

This is my cue to scream, *you don't know me*, and stomp out of the room. But instead I just lower my head.

"You know what my pop used to say? Charles and I would be whaling on each other, fighting. Man, we would really get into it. We broke the dining room table and tore the light right out of the ceiling once. Another time we barrel-rolled right through the front-room window and didn't even pause to pick the glass out of our teeth, we just kept up pounding on each other. Pop took us both by the ear, and I thought he was going to clap our heads together, but he didn't. He was burned up, don't get me wrong. My pop was a powerful man and he could'a taken us both to the woodshed. But this time he had a different look, practically had tears in his eyes. I can see his face clear as day. His cheeks was quivering. Said we didn't have to act that way. Said that we was safe, and when people's safe, they got room to be kind to each other."

I don't correct his grammar. "So you stopped fighting?"

"Nah. But he gave me something to think about. Some things are just too puny to fight about, you know? Like, if I'm safe, then why do I need to be mixing it up with some guy who looked at me wrong? Ain't worth it. See what I mean?"

I lick the last of the graham cracker crumbs off my finger. "So are you saying I'm safe?"

"Ain't you?" Only he really says, "Ain't chew?" That makes me think of Inga, who taught me to notice how people turn the word *you* into *chew*.

In a world with slam books, the H-bomb, commies and Nazis, and a box of books under my bed that could get Mom and me sent to jail, am I safe? I don't have the Thought Police looking in my windows like that guy Winston in *1984*. No one's actually dropping bombs on my head.

It could be I'm safe. It's hard to be sure.

Mom's moving around in the kitchen, so I whisper, "If you want another book, you know," I roll my eyes upward to point at my room, "ask me. You don't have to snoop around." Frank nods and gives me half a smile, which is probably all he can manage, given his banged-up face. Then in a loud voice I ask, "You want me to pour you a glass of milk?"

"Don't mind if I do," says Frank. "Unless you pouring something stronger."

"I heard that," Mom calls from the kitchen. Frank and I look straight at each other. He nods at the book bag and I hurry to stuff all the contents back inside before I have to explain the slam book to Mom. She comes in and Frank and I both smile up at her like nothing's going on.

"Oh, cripes, Frank. Every time I look at you, all I can think is how close you came to—oh, never mind. I'm just glad you're on the mend." Mom stands over us, drying her hands.

"Marjorie, would you run the vacuum around the living

215

room for me, quick like a little bunny? Mrs. Kovacs won't be here until next week, and I want the place to look nice when that man visits your father. He's coming first thing Sunday morning. No time for cleaning tomorrow. Full day—the auto show, then Greektown Pizza."

Tomorrow is opening day of the first Detroit Auto Show since the war, and it's a big deal. Fifty thousand people are supposed to be there. All the auto companies will be showing off their new designs. The papers and television have been full of stories on what to expect. Dad has free tickets through his work.

"And put this book bag up in your room. There won't be any homework until Sunday. I don't want to look at that on the table."

"What man is coming by?" asks Frank.

I know the man Mom's talking about. Mr. Scholtz, Inga's father. Tomorrow is Saturday. The next tomorrow is Sunday.

"Maybe the man forgot," I offer.

"Probably he didn't forget, Marjorie, so make your mother happy and vacuum, will you?"

"What man?"

"Oh, some man Jack thinks he might have maybe, I don't know exactly, might have known in the war, I guess." Mom twists a dish towel in her hands, and I am thinking that maybe this conversation is less about the vacuuming than it is about preparing Frank for Mr. Scholtz's visit.

"Some guy from the VFW? Big Daddy don't hang out there."

"Oh, not exactly. It's just a man he thought he might like to have a conversation with."

216

"A man from where? Work? The hardware store? Under the bridge?" Frank turns in his chair and tries to casually put his broken arm up on the table, but he can't lift it that high and gently puts it back down. His lips are curled up either from pain or frustration with Mom's hedging around.

"Oh, you know that little girlfriend of Margie's who came from Canada?" Mom reaches into the china cabinet and pulls out some of the good coffee cups and starts to wipe the dust out of them with her towel. She doesn't look directly at Frank, but takes little side-glances at him as she works. "Her father is stopping by on Sunday morning."

"The Kraut? Here?" Frank stands, his feet apart in a ready position. Hard to tell what he's ready for, but he's ready. "A Nazi? In this house?"

"Oh, Frank. We don't know that."

"Will he be bringing Little Miss Hitler Youth with him?"

"I have no idea, but Inga would have been just a toddler during the war, same as Marjorie."

"Inga's coming?" I ask, trying to not let my panic show. It makes my throat tighten to think about it.

"I have no answers to these questions, kids. Dad extended the invitation. I'm just the one making the coffee—and making sure the house is pulled together. Marjorie?"

"Okay, Mom."

"So that's it?" Frank slaps the table with his good hand.

Mom pulls her towel into a closed fist and places it on the table. "That is definitely it, Frank. This is Jack's idea, and we are not going to interfere in any way or make a scene."

"Well, we'll see about that," says Frank with a sniff. "I tell you what's a good idea. How about I ask my buddies Sam Kennedy and Mac Barone to pay that den of Nazis a visit with a couple a bricks and a torch? Just give me an address. Better yet, I'll draft Barry Goldberg and some of his boys. They won't mind getting their hands dirty. Show those Krauts we don't want their kind in this neighborhood. How 'bout we see about that?"

"We will not see anything of the kind," Mom lets go of her towel and bangs her bare fist on the table like a gavel. The china cups jump in their saucers. "How would you have liked it if Jack had just said, 'We'll see,' when you were lying in a hospital outside of Jackson? How about if I just say, 'We'll see' the next time you ask me when's dinner? *We'll see* is not an acceptable answer when you are part of this family, is that clear?"

There is something steely in Mom's voice, an edge that cuts sharply through the shafts of late afternoon sunlight coming in the window.

"No war goes on forever, Frank. Afterwards, the living take care of the living. The dead and the hate and the past, that takes care of itself." She sighs. "Or it should."

Frank shakes his head, poking his lower lip out in a pinched-up pout. "It's time to take a stand against them types, thinking they can take over the neighborhood like they tried to take over Europe."

Mom moves within spitting distance of Frank's broken face. She looks up and points her finger at his chin. "You are not listening to me, young man. You pull something like that, you won't have to wait for the police or Jack to come after you. I'll pound the snot out of you myself."

My eyes are so wide they're like dry plates. Mom's never talked like this before. To anyone. I think Frank must be surprised too, because he shuts up, just watching her.

Mom sniffs and says, "Yes. Then. Okay." She straightens the front of her apron and takes a half a step back. "Jack's invited that man to our home, and you will shake hands and act civil or," she hesitates, her jaws and lips tight, "or else. You understand me?"

Frank stomps across the wooden floor of the dining room, making the cups on the table dance and rattling the entire contents of the china cabinet. He pulls open the basement door and disappears with a slam. Then he opens the door and slams it again for emphasis.

Mom's glare falls on me.

"I'm moving," I say, slinging my book bag over my shoulder.

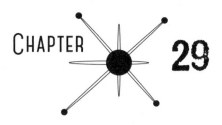

CHAPTER 29

"You have a lot more going for you than a pretty face," Mom says as she pulls open the door to Greektown Pizza, shuffling Carol Anne in ahead of her out of the blistering cold. Dad and Frank are parking the car.

The Detroit Auto Show had been like nothing I had ever seen before. Live music. Balloons. Models in evening dresses. It was a picture of what the future was going to look like, and the future was two-toned cars. Some of next season's cars were set on pedestals rotating under spotlights. Some were displayed, doors wide open, on the floor where you could stand in line to slide in behind the wheel and imagine yourself cruising down Woodward Avenue.

We all had our favorites. Dad's was the 1955 Thunderbird, a brand new sports car from Ford. It had a hard top convertible, a V8 engine, and something called jet tube taillights. Dad said he could go zero to sixty in that before you could blink twice. It has an automatic, but it also has a manual override for peeling out. After sliding into the driver's seat, Dad whined his way through all three imaginary gears to demonstrate how fast the car would perform off the line.

"Always been a Chrysler man, but this car's enough to turn

me traitor. That's one fine machine." Dad kept looking over his shoulder at the T-Bird as we wandered away.

Some sales guy tried to steer Mom to a station wagon with genuine wood paneling on the sides, but she would have nothing to do with that. Instead she had her eye on a black Chrysler Imperial with whitewall tires big as full moons.

"If you're going to dream, dream big!" she said, running her hands over the leather seats and checking out the electric windows. The trunk was so big on that car, I could have had a sleepover party in it and still had room left over.

Carol Anne didn't care what kind of car it was as long as it was red, and she kept Mom running after her from one side of the exhibition hall to the other as she pointed them all out.

My favorite was the two-toned, baby blue and white 1955 Chevy Bel Air convertible with its brand new sleek back end that looked like fins. It was the most modern of all the new designs as far as I was concerned. It made the rest of the cars at the show look like they had old-fashioned bubble butts. I could just see myself gliding out of that car in front of school. If any car could make someone automatically popular, it would be this car. Plus, the radio had push buttons. I tried it as loud as I could until the salesman growled, "Keep it down, sister."

But Frank was the one who really fell in love. He must have stood in line fifteen times to sit in the bucket seat with his hand on the gearshift of a new design from General Motors called the Corvette. It's a sports car, same as the new Thunderbird, but smaller and closer to the ground, more like a real racecar. It's light and small with a V6 engine and two-speed Powerglide transmission with the shifter on the floor. Priced at $3,498, it cost almost as much as a loaded Cadillac. Mom wondered what good any car was if you couldn't squeeze two brown grocery bags into the back.

Dad just sniffed and said General Motors had tried to introduce this toy car in New York last fall and it was a total flop. He didn't think the improvements amounted to diddly-squat in the new design and wondered what the engineers were drinking the day they came up with the idea of a plastic car body. The salesman tried to explain it was made of something called fiberglass, but Dad just sniffed at that. "Plastic's plastic. I was born late but not stupid." He said the Corvette was like putting a jet engine in a carnival kiddie car, and with an engine that size, a man wants some car around him for protection.

None of that mattered to Frank, though. He had stars in his eyes and a broken heart when we had to leave the Corvette behind.

Practically every new car at the Auto Show had a beautiful model standing alongside in a sparkly gown, her sweeping arms in long gloves. The new Cadillac had two, twins who were there to help demonstrate the car's dual exhaust system. All the models wore movie star dresses that swept the floor when they rotated. Some of them were wrapped in clouds of netting or draped in lace. Some of the dresses opened at the back in a V shape almost to the waistline, and others rose in high collars to frame their faces. Each one looked like she had just stepped out of a magazine in high heels with pointed toes that had been dyed to match her dress. Not a magazine like *Good Housekeeping* or *National Geographic*, but the magazines that Bernadette and I try to sneak peeks of at the library or Stewart's Drugstore. Huge magazines with titles like *Vogue* and *Town & Country*. They even wore eye makeup with black lines painted where their eyebrows were supposed to be, and red-lipped smiles were fixed on their perfect faces. They were the most glamorous women I had ever seen.

"Your daughter thinks she wants to be a model," Mom announces to Dad when he and Frank shake off their snowy coats and slide into our booth.

"What's this?" Dad asks.

Frank snorts, "Squirt wants to be a model. Right." I try to kick him under the table, but he's too fast for me and lifts his feet up, laughing.

Even though I hate him, I laugh, too. It's been a magical day, looking at a future all polished and shiny and ready to take off from the starting line. The kind of day when you think anything's possible.

After we put our order in, Mom excuses herself to go chat with Mrs. Papadopoulos, who's working at the cash register. I see both of them bend over a notebook that Mrs. P. pulls out of a drawer. She holds a pencil in her hand, and it looks like she's counting down some kind of list while Mom watches, nodding.

That's about the books! I think to myself. Mrs. P. is the president of the Friends of the Library. I want to run over and ask, but I don't want to give Mom away in case I'm right. Only I know I am right.

"We're just doing a favor for Mrs. P.," Mom had said when she dragged the box into the house and slid it under my bed. How many other women were doing her favors? She must have books stashed under beds all over town. When Mr. P. starts to walk their way, the notebook quickly disappears back into the drawer.

A secret list! What would Nancy Drew make of that? My rabbit ears go up and I lean toward the counter trying to pick up some clues to confirm what I'm pretty sure they're talking about.

Mom stretches over the counter to coo at the new baby, who's asleep in a basket on a shelf under the counter. And then I see Mrs. P. and Mom shake hands. Not a little finger touch like most women do. They nod at each other and shake hands like men, arms extended, two hard shakes.

"What's that all about?" asks Dad when Mom comes back to our table.

"Oh, a little new mother advice," Mom says casually. "That sweet baby is the cutest thing in ten states."

"It didn't look like you two were exchanging baby pictures." Dad's eyes linger over by the cash register where another family stands, paying their bill.

"I'm going to be Amelia Air-hurt when I grow up," announces Carol Anne. "And I'm going to drive a red Cadillac." ·

"Well, listen to that," says Dad, his attention brought back to the table. "Good for you, sweet pea."

"You girls are going to have so many more opportunities in the second half of this century," smiles Mom. "It's a new day. The walls are coming down."

"What walls are you talking about, Lila?" Dad asks.

Mom just smiles, and says, "Mark my words, change is coming." This is where Mom might have been quiet, but something about today and being out at a restaurant seems to have opened her up. She sits straight and tall and nods, folding her arms, lips spread tightly over her teeth in the littlest smile, as if she can see what the rest of us cannot. Then she reaches out to grab my hand and Carol Anne's at the same time, "You girls. You are never going to be trapped by some women's jobs section in the newspaper." She hesitates before she gives our hands one last squeeze. "You girls are going to fly." As she lets go of us, she nods again, firm as her handshake with Mrs. P.

"Like Amelia Air-hurt," Carol Anne pipes in.

"Oh, for sure you want to turn out like her," Frank grins.

"I tell you what I think," Dad says. "They're predicting that gasoline's going to jump to over thirty cents a gallon one of these days, and you girls better catch yourself a rich one. Ain't that right, George?" Dad shouts across the restaurant to Mr. P., whose big belly is covered by an apron that used to be white. He's so splattered with pizza sauce he looks like he's been shot in forty places.

"Marry rich! Is what my papa tell my sisters. But do they listen? Ohee! No! Now they live like paupers. They say they happy, but they poor like rats in a church."

"Church mice," Dad laughs.

"'Zactly," nods Mr. P., wiping tables.

When the pizza arrives, we dig in.

My brain is pizza pie loaded with everything. Shiny chrome

bumpers, satin dresses, and secret notebooks. I wonder how much it would hurt to pull my eyebrows out one hair at a time and then paint them back on again. I wonder how many secret notebooks there are in the world—Bernadette started one. Mom and Mrs. P. have one. Winston in the book *1984* had a really dangerous one. I wonder what I'll do if there isn't a section for me in the newspaper when I grow up. I'm not sure I want to fly. I definitely don't want to wind up lost and probably dead like Amelia Earhart. I wonder if they say, "She did not die by natural causes," if someone crashes a plane? I wonder how hard Frank would kick me under the table if I ask that question, or if he would just look sad, which would be much worse.

I reach for a second piece of pizza.

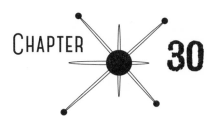

CHAPTER 30

Waiting on the porch is a man wearing a plaid shirt buttoned up to the neck.

It's Sunday and it's time.

The man's jacket's open, and he's holding a folded black wool cap in one hand, slapping it against the other hand, looking out at the street. I grab a glimpse of him through the peephole in the door.

It is one of those March mornings when the whole world decides to melt. Carol Anne is packing up some stuffed animals to go play at her friend Harriet's. Our house is so quiet you can hear the gutters drip. Water runs down the windows. If the sky weren't Superman blue, you'd swear it was raining.

When I saw him turn up the front walk, I ran to the peephole before he could ring the bell. He's alone, and he doesn't look dangerous. No uniform. No high officer's cap. Hardly any hair, definitely no horns. No *Sieg Hiel* with a one armed salute. He doesn't even look mysterious. He just looks like a guy my dad might know.

Even though it's eleven in the morning, the appointed time, I start to doubt the man on the porch is Mr. Scholtz. I might make him out to be a DP, but he definitely doesn't look like a Nazi. He isn't even wearing polished boots, just dusty work shoes.

Suddenly, he turns and I think maybe he looks me in the eye. I duck just as he rings the doorbell.

I don't have to call for Dad; he's right beside me with his hand on the doorknob as soon as the bell rings. "Move aside, there, private," he says to me before exploding into a hearty hello. "Scholtz, Scholtz. Come right in." Dad swings the door wide. "Welcome."

Mr. Scholtz jams his cap into his jacket pocket and shakes Dad's hand, nodding briskly. Mom enters the hallway. Introductions are made, but Mr. Scholtz doesn't make a move to take off his coat until Mom asks to take it from him.

"I thought maybe you might bring Inga with you," says Mom, smoothing his coat over her arm.

"Nah. Thank you. She stays at home. Help out her mama." Mr. Scholtz looks at me and smiles. "You sit with my Inga at school, yes?" His English is better than Inga's and his voice is soft and velvety. He does not click his heels together and he's not barking orders at anyone. He's not like any German I have ever seen before in the movies or on television.

I nod and then look at my feet. I wonder if I look as guilty as I feel. I do sit with Inga, but we haven't exactly been best friends the last couple of weeks. In fact, we haven't been talking at all.

"Marjorie tells us she's a very sweet girl," Mom says.

"Yah." Mr. Scholtz nods in agreement. "Smart, too."

"Marjorie says she speaks French." Mom's just making conversation to be nice. I can tell that it's working. Mr. Scholtz smiles and runs his fingers through his hair. His head bobs up and down as he tells her, "Yah. French, German, a little Russian, now English."

Russian? Inga speaks Russian? Wait until Bernadette and Mary Virginia get a load of that. Not only is Inga a Nazi, she also can speak the language of the commies? She's doomed. I wonder—what else don't I know about Inga?

"Who's this little one?" Mr. Scholtz asks, bending to look at Carol Anne, who flashes out from behind Mom's skirt before disappearing again.

"Carol Anne," we all say at the same time. With that, Carol Anne darts from the hall and into the dining room. This breaks the ice a little and everyone laughs, except me.

"Come in. Let's have a seat in the living room here. Lila, we'll take some of that coffee you made. You take your coffee black?" asks Dad.

"Straight coffee, not light," says Mr. Scholtz.

"Spoken like a good soldier," says Dad. "No cream and sugar baloney in the field, right?"

"Jawohl," says Mr. Scholtz.

"Frank," Dad bellows. Mom and Dad exchange glances. You kind of have to know them to understand that they are talking to each other, because no words are said. But I know what they're doing. Will Frank come up and meet Mr. Scholtz? Will he act polite or snort and paw the ground, ready to charge?

"I'll call him up, you two go on and have a seat," Mom says.

I silently shadow them into the living room, slide onto a footstool, and fold my hands. Motionless, I pretend I am part of the living room set. Mom calls, "Frank," her voice sweet and musical.

The back door opens and closes. Exit Carol Anne. The waiting continues.

The clock on the mantel ticks. Mr. Scholtz makes a comment about today's warmer temperatures.

"Mother Nature's giving us a break, that's for sure," Dad nods. He scratches the back of his neck.

Silence rushes in to fill the spaces between their words. Tick. Tick.

Dad clears his throat as if he's going to say something, but he doesn't. Mr. Scholtz puts his hands in his pockets. He's taking in the whole room. He strides over to the fireplace.

Dad stands behind his chair, running his hands back and forth across the back of it. He's watching Mr. Scholtz. Not directly, but in little glances.

Mr. Scholtz leans in to examine the face of the mantel clock. "Is German made, this clock."

"Family piece. From the wife's grandparents." Dad moves across the room to the fireplace.

"See, here?" Mr. Scholtz points.

Dad squints up close to the clock. "Well, what do you know?" Dad answers. Silence interrupts the conversation again. I look around the room, wondering what they can talk about next.

Then stomping on the basement stairs. *Bam-bam-bams*, louder with every step. Like a sledgehammer slowly driving in a post. *Bam. Bam.* I look at the drapes, expecting them to shudder. Or the pictures to fall off the wall. But nothing moves. Frank stands in the doorway.

"Ah, here we go. Here's the final member of the family." Dad makes introductions and watches Frank's good arm, willing it to shake Mr. Scholtz's outstretched hand. It takes a few seconds longer than natural, but Frank stiffly sticks out his hand.

"Good. Good," Dad says, pointing at chairs for Frank and Mr. Scholtz. Then to me he says, "We're going to have some man talk here, kid."

This is my signal to go to my room and leave them alone. But I want to hear everything. I want to know how this man in the plaid shirt traveled from "the field" to our living room. My entire life, Germans have been the evil enemy, but this man looks about as evil as the ice-cream man. Frank sits beside the fireplace, stiff as the poker, shovel, and broom standing in the brass holder next to him.

I hold perfectly still. My eyes are begging, but all Dad does is point at the stairs and say, "March!"

I drag my reluctant feet up the stairs, stomp my way across the bedroom floor and make the bed squeak when I bounce on it. Then quickly, I slide my shoes off and tiptoe back across the room to take a seat at the top of the stairs where I won't miss a word.

"Well, I'll be damned. A Panzer man. You bet. I was in Patton's army. Following Rommel, were you? Hell of a general."

Mr. Scholtz's voice is ten times softer than my dad's. I can barely make out his part of the conversation, but it sounds like they have something in common since they were both in tanks in the war. Or kind of in common. They were on different sides. Part of me leans forward so I can hear better and part of me's ready to run to call the police in case Frank starts a fight. But so far, he says nothing.

"Officer?" I hear Mr. Scholtz ask.

"Went in a private and came out a lieutenant. Battlefield commission. You all shot just about every one of my commanders. So one day, they hang a bar on me in the middle of a muddy field, and I'm an officer." Dad laughs like someone told him a big joke. "Those Panzers packed a heck of a punch. No doubt about it." There are gaps in their talking. The polite rattle of cups on saucers.

"I was in Sherman tanks across Africa, into Italy," Dad says.

"They hot, the Shermans?"

Dad laughs. "Hotter than the fires of hell. Your tanks have one of those little fans that didn't do squat? And we couldn't take down the armor for a breath of air because your guns never let up."

"I am a big man before the war." Mr. Scholtz's voice. "I lose ten kilo." He's laughing, too.

"Sweat boxes! We thought you had us when those Panzer IVs showed up. Fast. Man, the only way we could get off an engine shot was to circle around and attack from the rear. That there Panzer IV was faster than any Sherman."

Between his accent and the softness of his voice, I can hardly make out anything Mr. Scholtz is saying until he starts making *boom boom* noises.

"Oh, yeah," says Dad. "We had the airpower. If we hadn't controlled the air after Normandy, you would have had us gun to gun."

Is Dad saying the Germans might have won the war? I never heard anyone even hint that the Americans weren't the winners all the way. I'm thinking about this new information when I hear Dad say he thinks he knows where he can lay his hands on some maps. Just as he tells Mr. Scholtz to sit tight, I spring from my spot at the top of the stairs and fly to my bed. Dad leaps up the stairs two at a time and appears in my doorway.

"I need to take a look at your box of maps." He drops to his knees as if he's about to dive under my bed. I beat him to it.

"I'll get it," I say. The last thing I need is for Dad to pull out the wrong box.

Dad's eyes fix on my neat piles of maps and brochures. "Zowie, kid. That's quite a collection there. You got a map of Africa?"

"The Congo?" I ask. "British Kenya? Ethiopia? South Africa?"

"Northern Africa. Not that I expect you to know these countries, but Morocco? Egypt?"

I start pulling out maps. "You want Tunisia, too?" I ask him.

"Yeah, kid. I want Tunisia. You're just full of surprises. How 'bout Greece? Italy? Good gravy, Marjorie. Czechoslovakia? Yep. Here, give me all you got for Europe." And he's gone with half of my map collection.

"Wait till you get a load of this," he says, his feet drumming down the stairs.

For the next two hours they talk over those maps. Who

was where, when. Whose tank was stuck in the mud and how deep. Why a British starched shirt named Montgomery wouldn't engage. Which army left its flank open. Where they both were positioned in the Battle of the Bulge. The cracking of the Siegfried Line. West Germany. Austria. They even talk about the weather.

I wonder if Inga knows what her dad did in the war, if he talks to her about it. I wonder what it was like when he came home from the war.

Paper confetti rained down on parades of GIs when they arrived back in New York City. That's what happens when you win a war. You get your picture in *Life* magazine, waving from ships or kissing pretty girls in the street. First New Yorkers line up for a parade and then your hometown puts you in a convertible and parades you around again. All the GIs got that after they won the war. I've seen the pictures a hundred times.

But what happens when you lose a war? For sure, no one throws you a parade. Do you just go home and pick up where you left off? What if your home's not there anymore? Lots of German towns were bombed flat, nothing but a few broken-down walls left. Do you just forget about the place that used to be home and find somewhere else to live? Do you move to Canada?

"Capture here," I hear Mr. Scholtz say. "Schwarze Soldaten. How you say?"

"Black soldiers! You were picked up by the 761st Tank Battalion. Well, I'll be damned."

"Different American army."

"Same army, just separate. Separate mess halls, separate quart-

234

ers. All kinds of stories swirling around those GIs. Cornpones from Iowa saying that blacks have horns and tails. They howl at night. Plain ignorance. You know, Patton didn't think the blacks had it in them, but I knew better. Yep. Played football at East High School in Akron, Ohio, with Negroes and I knew they could hit hard as a white boy. I heard of that battalion—their motto was 'Come out fighting.' Guess you caught the business end of that stick, eh?"

Patton. Rommel. Montgomery. The tank commanders' names are as familiar to me as the characters in *Alice in Wonderland*, real and unreal at the same time. General Patton was in charge of the American tanks, General Montgomery was in charge of the British, and General Rommel was in charge of the Germans. I know they were real people, but I have only heard about them in stories. To me they are as fictional as the Queen of Hearts, who waves her wand and says, "Off with their heads."

Would Inga know those names just like she knew about *Curious George*? The more they talk, the more I wish Mr. Scholtz had brought her along, even though it would make Bernadette's head explode if she heard that Inga had come to my house after I'd signed the loyalty oath. I start making a mental list of questions for Inga. So many questions, I might have to write them down. But not in the slam book. Definitely not there.

The questions in the slam book are stupid questions with made-up answers. I have real questions. Like, do you just hide in the basement when a war breaks out in your neighborhood? Mom says we had food rationing during the war, with stamps and books. Did they do that in Germany? What happens in a war if the grocery store's bombed out? Where do you buy bananas? Do they close school when there's a war? Do people go to church on Sunday, or do they wait for Monday if there are too many bombs?

Was her dad different before the war than he was after, like Frank's pop? Is it easier or harder to turn back into a normal person after you've won a war or lost a war? How do you become a normal person again after being a Nazi?

And what happened to her brother?

Dad's voice interrupts the stream of questions rat-a-tat-tatting in my head. "Maybe they should have set up a boxing ring and let the three of 'em have at it so the rest of us grunts could go home." Dad laughs.

I sit and listen at the top of the stairs until my forehead hurts from squinting to hear their words. A lot of their conversation makes no sense to me. I don't know if it would make sense to Inga, but I'd sure like to talk about it with her.

And she would, too. I know she would. She would talk to me, and I would listen and then not tell anyone if she didn't want me to. And I have the feeling she would keep my secrets, too. I remember the scared rabbit look in her eye that first day, and how she trusted me. I wonder if she could trust me again.

I go downstairs to pour a glass of milk because it's a good excuse to peek into the living room. Dad doesn't even notice me. A dozen maps are spread out all over the floor, and he and Mr. Scholtz are on their knees. The coffee cups sit abandoned on top of the television, open beer bottles on the floor. Even Frank's leaning forward, cradling his busted arm, though he hasn't left his chair.

I walk slowly back to my room. When the front door opens, I hear more laughter and good-byes. Dad tells Mr. Scholtz to "Keep it on the road," and Mr. Scholtz tells him to "Rest easy."

Rest easy? I race down the stairs just as Dad holds up one hand in a final wave. He taps his eyebrow with one finger, almost in a loose salute.

Mr. Scholtz lifts the black cap above his head in a wave. The scary commie spy cap. The same cap I saw hanging on the hook at Inga's house. The cap he stood twisting in his hands on our front porch earlier. He slaps it on and taps the brim with one finger. He turns and starts walking down the sidewalk.

Frank stands at the front picture window, one arm in its sling, the other in a triangle propped on his hip. Silent. So silent I wonder if he's breathing.

Dad and I stand inside the glass storm door. Dad puts his arm across my shoulders. The house gutters are dripping, and the snow glistens and streams toward the sewers under the brilliant sun. The back door opens and closes. I hear Carol Anne burbling in the kitchen, home from Harriet's house. The front yard's almost grassy again, except for the U-shaped snow mound where our fort used to be.

"Your friend's papa, he's a good man. A good soldier." Dad says, his head nodding.

I look up at my dad and try to smile. I nod, too, because all my whole forever life I've been told what a good soldier is. A good soldier doesn't cry. Keeps his chin up and doesn't pull a face when there's work to do.

Mr. Scholtz is a good soldier?

I lick my lips. A thousand questions pound on my eardrums. One question booms the loudest. I don't know if it's a question that's okay to ask, or if it's something I'm not supposed to talk about, like the box of books under my bed. This question is the one written the most in the slam book. It's what everyone wants to know.

"Daddy?" I clear my throat. "Was Mr. Scholtz a Nazi?"

Dad looks out the door and is silent for only half a breath.

"War's over, kid."

"Yeah, but—"

"That's it." He pats my shoulder twice.

Frank scuffs behind us, heading into the kitchen. His head's down. Stuff's got to be simmering in him, too. He drifts along like a shadow, saying nothing. For once, I wish he would say something. Anything.

I can't let it go, even if Dad did say, "That's it."

"But you were in a war with him, Daddy."

"Yup. Soldiers work to make the war and then we got to try and make the peace. That's how it goes, little darlin'," he pauses. "You see what I see?"

I look, but Mr. Scholtz has turned the corner and is out of sight.

"Right there, in the drive. You see those salt stains on our car?"

"Yeah," I say, though the car looks perfectly clean to me. Just like it always is, polished and shining in the sun, the whitewall tires glowing.

"I say we get to work and wash that car before the salt eats clean through the fender. Be a good soldier and run to the basement and grab me the pail, will you? Weather's giving us a break today. Might as well take advantage of it."

"Okay," I say, but I don't move.

My dad looks down at me, "Sport? Don't just stand there, lead, follow, or—"

I know what he's about to say, so I say it first. "Or get out of the way."

"That's my girl. Now make up your mind, and get it in gear."

I start for the basement and then change my mind. I turn and dash up the stairs to my room.

"Hey, sport, where you off to?"

"I'll get the bucket. Gimme a sec." I bolt into my room and tear open my book bag. I grab the slam book and bolt back down both flights of stairs, all the way to the basement. The bucket is sitting beside the washing machine where it always is, but I turn to the furnace.

I am not allowed to touch the furnace. Ever. It sits like a black iron mountain in the corner of the basement. And I am definitely not allowed to creak open the grate and expose the orange flames. But I have watched Dad open it hundreds of times and know to first pull down the asbestos mitt from its hook and slip my hand inside of it.

That's just what I do.

Then I jerk the latch to the side and swing wide the door.

Because of the higher temperatures outside today, the glowing coals are lying in a low pile instead of jumping in flames that lick out into the room when the grate swings open.

When the slam book hits the coals, it bursts into red and orange flames. I don't wait to see the words *Go Home* melt into the fire. I slam the door, but not before part of the warmth of the glowing coals seeps inside of me. I put the fireproof mitt back on its hook.

"Marjorie? You get lost?" Dad calls from the top of the stairs.

"I'm coming!" I shout. I grab the bucket and fly up the stairs.

I hand him the bucket. "I need to go tell Bernadette something," I say as I reach for my coat. He looks at me with a tip of his head. "I really need to, Daddy."

"You bugging out on me?"

"I'll be back soon. I promise. Carol Anne wants to help, don't you, Carol Anne?"

But I don't wait for her to answer. I don't touch the stairs as I launch off the porch, putting my coat on as I fly. I hear Mom's voice calling after me, but I keep running.

Lead, follow, or get out of the way. The words have a rhythm that carries me right up to Bernadette's front door. I repeat them in my head the whole way there. One foot *lead*, one foot *follow*, next step *get out of the way*, over and over, until I reach her front door.

Panting, I study the wooden door with its brass knocker. I could tap my knuckles against the storm door like I usually do, but instead I open it, reach up, and give the brass ring on the inside door a big whack. And then I whack it a couple more times. I let the storm door ease shut as I hear footsteps on the other side. It's Mrs. Ferguson's high heels.

As if the door is invisible, I can see her in her straight skirt and sweater set. I can see her pearls. I can see she doesn't want any part of what I am about to say in her house, and I just can't wait to say it.

"Marjorie, you scared the living daylights out of me," she says as she opens the inside door, leaving the storm door between us. Bernadette appears behind her.

"Marjorie?"

"It's too close to dinner to have your little friend over, Bernadette," says Mrs. Ferguson as she turns on her heel and disappears into the darkness of the house.

"You should have called first," Bernadette starts. But this conversation doesn't belong to her. It belongs to me.

Bernadette doesn't know that, and she looks down at my hands, opening the glass door a crack. "I thought maybe you were returning the slam book," she whispers. "I'm going to need it by tomorrow."

"I'm not returning the slam book," I say. "Not now, not ever."

"You have to," she says, her face pinched tight as a balloon knot. She leans into the outside air, "You *have* to."

"No, I don't, and besides, I can't," I answer. "I burned it up."

"What?"

"In the furnace. Burned to bits."

"But—"

"And now I'm going over to Inga's to tell her I'm sorry."

"What for? She doesn't know anything. We didn't give it to her yet."

"You think she's stupid because she's just learning English, but she's really good at French and German. She's not stupid, Bernadette. You don't know what she knows, and neither do I, but I'm going to find out and tell her I'm really, really sorry."

"But we didn't even decide if we were going to give the book to her. We have to ask everybody." Bernadette talks fast, as if she can undo what I did; only she can't.

"No, we don't. It's up in smoke."

"Are you saying you want to be friends with a Nazi?" Bernadette stands tall now.

"I'm saying I want to be friends with Inga."

"But you agreed. You agreed with everyone. You signed a loyalty oath, remember? We all did. You said she's not like us. I heard you, Marjorie."

I stop for a second on that one. "You're right," I answer. I look hard at Bernadette. I look into her so hard I can see the pigtailed, kindergarten-Bernadette, who I know still lives inside of her. "She's not like the rest of us . . . she's nice."

"But—"

"Nope. That's it, Bernadette." I turn to leave, balancing myself with both arms as I cross the porch to the steps that are shining wet with melting ice.

"But who are you going to walk to school with now?" she asks, the question comes out of her mouth like a slap. The door clicks closed.

Her words don't sting, though. Not one bit.

"I'll be out there at seven-forty-five same as always," I say. "You make up your mind."

I slip down the stairs, holding tight to the handrail. I feel Bernadette's eyes on my back, but don't turn around.

The storm door squeaks open again.

"Tomorrow?" she asks.

"Tomorrow and the next tomorrow." I turn partway around to answer, but I don't stop walking.

When I get to the end of her driveway, I wave to catch Dad's eye and point in the direction of Inga's house. Dad waves back with his soapy sponge.

War's over, kid . . .

With Dad's voice inside my head, my eyes travel down the sidewalk that will take me from Bernadette's house to Inga's.

Suddenly, it's as if I am hanging onto the side of the pool at swimming class. A familiar panic grips my lungs. For a second I think, *I can't do this. It's too scary. I'll never make it.*

I take in a gulp of air. The wind catches the hem of my coat, and I leap across the melting snow.

JULY 1957

Sara Holbrook, age eight

AUTHOR'S NOTE

This book is a work of fiction based on facts extracted from my memories and family stories and mixed with research. Let me try and sort through which is which, if such a thing is truly possible.

I was born after WWII, in 1949, and grew up during the 1950s in the northern suburbs of Detroit, a city segregated by both race and ethnicity. In Hamtramck, the shop and street signs were in Polish, and in Oak Park, they were in Hebrew. Eight Mile Road, before it was made famous by Eminem, served as the dividing line between black and white families. My neighborhood was close to Twelve Mile Road. It was a neighborhood of European immigrants and folks who had relocated from the South for jobs in the thriving auto industry.

Detroit in those days was a cultural olio. Many of the labels folks placed on one another in those days (DP, Polack, Jap, Kraut) were not necessarily used with the same degree of malice we associate with those terms today. Today, these terms are no longer acceptable. They reflect a past era, and they need to remain there.

Language, like society, is constantly evolving. It was in the mid-1980s when I heard a new term, "posttraumatic stress disorder," used to describe vets overcoming the stress of battle. I remember the day and where I was standing. I remember repeating the phrase aloud several times and then thinking to myself, "Wow, there's a term for that?"

The author's father, Lt. Wallace Scott Holbrook, beside a
Sherman tank, the Second Army of the United States,
12th Armored Division

The character of Jack is based on my father, Lt. Wallace Scott
Holbrook. He served as a tank commander in the 12th Armored
Division of the Second Army United States in the European Theater
of World War II. He received multiple Purple Hearts and the Silver
Star. After I was born, he was recalled to serve in Korea, where he
received more citations for bravery, including a Bronze Star with
a few clusters. The symptoms of his posttraumatic stress disorder
lessened as the years wore on, but until he died at sixty-five,

The author's mother, Suzanne McNeal Holbrook,
with Schlitzie

he would occasionally kick his way out of a troubled sleep or bolt from his chair and yell. He was buried in Arlington Cemetery in 1991.

Lila is very loosely based on my own mother, a college graduate who endured merciless teasing about her degree. Brilliant, she struggled in a changing but still stifling era for women. I have to add that my father evolved in his view of women and education over the years, happily celebrating my graduation years later from the same college my mother attended, now called the University of Mount Union. My childhood idol really was Nancy Drew. I'd never met a woman so independent, with her own roadster and no one telling her what to do. I wanted to be like that.

The fictional character of Inga was inspired by a friend from elementary school, an immigrant from Germany via Canada. Monica Holtzer, wherever you are, I remember you as a very nice person, indeed. And I remember one afternoon when our fathers met over maps in the living room. Every other detail about Inga and her family is fiction.

No soldier serves alone. Soldiers take their families with them, through war and peace, and sometimes, tragically, through the separation of death. A young man, orphaned by the suicide of his veteran father, did live in our basement for a year until he graduated and joined the service. I don't know where life took him afterwards. Other than that, the character of Frank is pure fiction.

I chose the winter of 1954 for this story because it was the climax of the McCarthy era, a time of simmering fear and suspicion. The enemy was everywhere, Nazis, commies, the Bomb. Fear permeated our libraries, our schools, our military, our political institutions. The first Detroit Auto Show after WWII happened that year on February 20, and on March 9, Edward R. Murrow released a fateful analysis of the McCarthy hearings on CBS. For narrative purposes, in this fictional account of the time, these two events take place in the same week, but in reverse order. That year, the Red Wings went on to win the Stanley Cup, two-toned cars revolutionized the American ride, and on June 9 of that year, Joseph N. Welch poked a pin in Senator Joseph McCarthy's swell of influence by asking him, "Have you no sense of decency, sir?" These facts, among others, I found through research.

Countries advertising in *National Geographic* really did send free travel brochures and maps to travel-hungry kids who sent in self-addressed stamped envelopes, and I had quite a collection. Today I can say I have visited over forty countries and counting.

What I have learned through all this is that you will never understand your parents until much later, niceness is worth defending with ferocity, and maybe most importantly, wishes really can come to life.

Sara Holbrook

Acknowledgments

So many to thank.

First, my tenacious editor, Carolyn Yoder, for believing in the book and for her careful assistance and insistence on making it better, thank you. And thanks to Boyds Mills Press and the Highlights Family for your continued support over the years.

No editor would have even looked at this manuscript, however, without the advice and feedback from so many readers, I am embarrassed and humbled to list them. Thank you, Emma Cigany, Maryanne Darr Norman, Stephanie Harvey, Sarah Willis and my pen-gal friends, Thrity Umigar, Loung Ung, Kristin Olsen, and Karen Sandstrom, and Paula McLain. Thanks to Sharon Draper for your unfailing encouragement, Pam Muñoz Ryan for your invaluable guidance, and Tony Romano for helping me over the finish line.

Thank you to all the English language learners I have taught and conversed with over the years whose voices I heard coming from the mouths of my fictional immigrants. Thank you especially to Johnny Ngo for teaching me about "tomorrow and the next tomorrow."

Thank you to my family, especially to my father's big brother, Lt. William C. Holbrook, who served bravely as a PBY rescue pilot in the Pacific and as my "'nother daddy" while my father was in Korea, and who did his best to help me understand.

And finally, to my travel partner in life, Michael Salinger. Thank you for your encouragement, your wicked sense of humor, your sage writing advice, and your assistance in navigating the motorbikes. You help me be brave.

Bibliography*

"1953 Ford Crestline Sunliner Convertible." Pack Automotive Museum.
http://www.packautomotivemuseum.com/c149.html.

Auto Brochures. "1955 Chevrolet." http://www.lov2xlr8.no/brochures/chevy/55chev/x55chev.html.

"1955 Chrysler & Imperial Brochure." Imperial Web Pages.
http://imperialclub.org/~imperialclub/Yr/1955/55Chrysler/index.htm.

"2014 Detroit Auto Show: How America's most important auto show has changed through the years: 1954 Detroit Auto Show." NY Daily News. http://www.nydailynews.com/autos/auto-shows/detroit-auto-show-gallery-1.1575210.

American Psychiatric Association. "PTSD." January 1, 2015.
http://www.psychiatry.org/ptsd.

Arlington National Cemetery. "Find A Grave—Millions of Cemetery Records and Online Memorials." February 1, 2012. http://www.findagrave.com/cgi-bin/fg.cgi?page=gr&GSln=Holbrook&GSfn=Wallace&GSiman=1&GScid=49269&GRid=85811148&.

---

* *Websites current at time of publication*

Brighton, Terry. "Bulging Ambitions." In *Masters of Battle: Monty, Patton and Rommel at War*. London: Penguin Books, 2009.

Davisson, Budd. "Piper Cub History Performance and Specifications." Piper Cub History Performance and Specifications. http://www.pilotfriend.com/aircraft%20performance/Piper/1.htm.

DeLong, Leslie, and Nancy W. Burkhart. "Ulcers and Ulcerlike Lesions." In *General and Oral Pathology for the Dental Hygienist*, 339. Baltimore, MD: Lippincott Williams & Wilkins, 2008.

"Edward R. Murrow: A Report on Senator Joseph R. McCarthy." Media Resources Center, Moffit Library, University of California, Berkeley. July 25, 2006. Accessed April 10, 2015. http://www.lib.berkeley.edu/MRC/murrowmccarthy.html

"'Farm Foolery'***Cartoon***." YouTube video, 1:42, Famous Studios, posted by "ChazingRainbows," December 3, 2011. 1949. https://www.youtube.com/watch?v=oXKzbTXuNKg&index=14&list=PLSaJZ25wG-gichkzHGhZXYOg0cdXfts5-.

Fried, Richard M. *Nightmare in Red: The McCarthy Era in Perspective*. 29–34, 135–136, 161–162. New York, New York: Oxford University Press, 1991.

Glass, Thomas. "The 925th Engineer Aviation Regiment in Germany." In *The Trials & Triumphs of A Regimental Commander During World War II*, 225. Victoria, British Columbia: Trafford Publishing, 2006.

Truman, Harry S. "Statement by the President Upon Signing the Displaced Persons Act," June 25, 1948. Online by Gerhard Peters and John T. Woolley, The American Presidency Project. http://www.presidency.ucsb.edu/ws/?pid=12942.

Hemmings. "1955-'57 Ford Thunderbird." February 1, 2006. http://www.hemmings.com/hmn/stories/2006/02/01/hmn_feature1.html.

Louie, Barbara G. "Travel." In *Northville Michigan*, 145. Dover, New Hampshire: Arcadia Publishers, 2001.

McNessor, Mike. "1953 Chevrolet Corvette Early Missteps Nearly Cut Short a 60-year Run." *Hemmings Motor News*, September 1, 2013.

Miller, Craig. "12th Armored Division." 12th Armored Division. Accessed May 6, 2016. 12tharmoredmuseum.com

Monahan, Evelyn, and Rosemary Neidel-Greenlee. *And If I Perish: Frontline U.S. Army Nurses in World War II*. New York, New York: Anchor Books: Division of Random House, 2004.

Morse, Joseph Laffan. *Unicorn Book of 1954*. Unicorn Books, 1955.

Murrow, Edward R. "Edward R. Murrow—See It Now (March 9, 1954)." YouTube video, 2:02, posted by "Justin Hillyard," August 22, 2009. https://www.youtube.com/watch?v=anNEJJYLU8M.

"PTSD: National Center for PTSD." January 1, 2015. http://www.ptsd.va.gov.

Rey, H. A. (Hans Augusto). *Curious George Rides a Bike*. Boston: Houghton Mifflin, 1952.

Robbins, Louise. *Censorship and the American Library: The American Library Association's Response to Threats to Intellectual Freedom, 1939–1969*. 22, 189. Westport, CT: Praeger, 1996.

Sasser, Charles W. *Patton's Panthers: the African-American 761st Tank Battalion in World War II*. New York: Pocket Books, 2014. 223-25.

Stall, David. "VictorySiren.com™ —The Internet Home of the Chrysler Air Raid Siren." January 1, 2003. http://www.victorysiren.com/x/index.htm.

Terkle, Studs. "Epilogue: Boom Babies and Other New People." In *The Good War*, 574-589. New York, New York: New Press; Reprint Edition, 1997.

"Trench Fever." *The American Heritage Medical Dictionary*. 2007, 2004. Houghton Mifflin Company. http://medical-dictionary.thefreedictionary.com/Trench+Fever.

"'The Big Flame Up' (Bouncing Ball Song: Hot Time in the Old Town Tonight Included!)." YouTube video, 7:28, Famous Studios, posted by "ChazingRainbows," December 8, 2011. 1949. https://www.youtube.com/watch?v=CeJLD-JSg-U&list=PLSaJZ25wG-gichkzHGhZXYOg0cdXfts5-.

Wall, Wendy. "Anti–Communism in the 1950s." The Gilder Lehrman Institute of American History. January 1, 2007. https://www.gilderlehrman.org/history-by-era/fifties/essays/anti-communism-1950s.

Wasserstein, Bernard. "European Refugee Movements After World War Two." BBC News. February 17, 2011. http://www.bbc.co.uk/history/worldwars/wwtwo/refugees_01.shtml.

Wikso, Ron. "Mr. Wizard Studios." January 1, 2004. http://www.mrwizardstudios.com.

Young, William H., and Nancy K. Young. "Television Soap Operas of the 1950s." In *The 1950s*, 227. Westport, Connecticut: Greenwood Press, 2004.

Zal, Pawel. "1952 Nash Rambler Deliveryman." Automobile Catalog. 2010. http://www.automobile-catalog.com/make/nash/rambler_1/rambler_1_deliveryman/1952.html.

Picture Credits

Photos courtesy of the author